HELL BORN

DEADWOOD SISTERS: THE UNLUCKY BOOK 1

Hellborn

Deadwood Sisters: The Unlucky Book 1

Cover Art: Atlantis Book Design

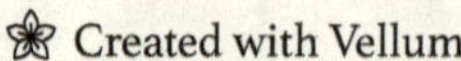
Created with Vellum

HELLBORN

Deadwood Sisters: The Unlucky Book 1

LISA MANIFOLD

To Val, Dennis, and Tim
The Holy Trinity of Docs

In 1876, John Henry Holliday, known as Doc Holliday, spent part of the year living in Deadwood, South Dakota. He'd come to work in the newly opened Bella Union Saloon. Doc left Deadwood in 1877, never to return. As far as he knew, he didn't leave anything behind.
He was wrong

PROLOGUE

Deadwood, South Dakota

1912

Desdemona Nightingale Burns—she'd kept her husband's last name even though she had no idea where he'd gone; even though she knew he was finally on the other side—walked through the house with a single candle. Everything was different now that her mother had died. For example, if her mother was gone, why was someone—or something—banging around in her mother's room? She'd ignored it until she could ignore the noise no longer, and headed out to investigate.

For thirty-six years, ever since her mother had fallen in love with—and lost—John Holliday, she'd presided over the house on Main Street. Her mother, also Desdemona Nightingale but known as Granny Nightingale, had won the house in a card game shortly after Holliday blew out of town with the wind. She claimed it was one of the two great gifts Holliday had left her with as he'd been teaching her to gamble before he disappeared. The other was herself. Not that anyone knew. As far as the world was concerned, John Henry "Doc" Holliday had died without issue.

She and her mother had worked hard to keep it that way.

The man who'd lost the house had done his best to win it back, but Granny Nightingale prevailed. She fixed it up and raised her daughter there, married and lost a husband—who, like her own, was practically forgotten--and recently, opened a tea and herbal shop. Desdemona made sure her mother was careful. After all, Granny was a witch, and no one needed to know. That's what she told her girls. Everything was all right, for now. When the girls got older—when they stopped getting older—it would become more difficult. She had enough problems with her own lack of aging. Add four more girls? Desdemona shook her head. No need to borrow trouble until it happened. With four daughters, she'd be able to claim all sorts of nieces as the years went on.

After all, people saw what they wanted to see. If the Nightingales were polite, quiet, paid taxes, didn't look at anyone's husband, they would be safe.

Even if there were lingering looks from the husbands, a quick spell from Granny would take care of that. She sent a prayer to the goddess. That was something else she'd have to take on. She was the matriarch now. Her mother didn't want to go, but she'd decided to leave. She wanted to make it easier for her daughter and granddaughters.

But to her, it felt like there was something else, some other reason her mother had decided to leave. She'd always told Desdemona that she'd stay around until everyone wanted her to leave.

I didn't want you to leave, she thought.

None of them had to die. Not unless they wanted to. As long as they stayed in Deadwood, the Nightingales could live as long as they wished. Desdemona wasn't sure it was a gift. For the most part, it seemed to incur more work. Her personal thought was that her mother was tired, and this was a good excuse. Along with whatever it was her mother was hiding.

She lifted the candle higher as she stood outside of the door where her mother—known to one and all, even her, as Granny—had slept recently. There it was again. The knocking sound that had dragged her out of bed.

Desdemona sent a silent prayer to the goddess that her mother had not decided to haunt them. She said it silently in case Granny was, in fact, still around. Carefully, she opened the door, and walked in with the candle held out in front of her.

The smell of Overholt rye whiskey hit her like a brick to the face. She was familiar with it because Granny set out a glass every year on November eighth, the day John Holliday supposedly died. She swore it was his drink of choice, and as she'd met him when he worked at the Bella Union, Granny was in a position to know.

Desdemona hated the smell. She wondered if Granny had a bottle hidden somewhere that had broken in the confusion of the funeral.

"Hello, darlin'," a male voice drawled. "It's about time we met."

CHAPTER ONE

The sound of breaking china echoed around the house as I slammed out the front door. I made sure to slam the screen door hard, just to make a point.

"Damn woman," I muttered.

"I heard that!"

"Good!" I yelled over my shoulder. "I wanted you to!" I stomped to my car, pulling my keys from my pocket. As I got into the car, I pulled my hair up into a messy bun. I caught sight of myself in the mirror. Dark brown hair, brownish green eyes, and the nose ring. I couldn't get used to it, but I needed it to look like someone else. The only thing that would cure me now was to race down the road in my Porsche 911. Speed was a universal healer.

Or killer, if you weren't careful. But it didn't matter. I couldn't die. More's the damn pity. The nose ring sparkled in the sunlight. Having to look like someone else was one of the joys of not being able to die. "I hate my life!" I made sure to yell out the window.

"I heard that!" came from the house again.

As I gunned the engine, I saw our neighbor, Mrs. Kittrick,

glaring. She hated us. And for this, she'd probably call the cops. Noise complaints were her favorite bitch move. Like we didn't have Sturgis here every damn year. But gotta call the po-po on those Nightingale ... women.

That's how she referred to us. Those Nightingale...women. You could feel the pause. I knew that she wanted to call us whores. But she couldn't bring herself to do it. As the supposed daughter of myself, I was another one in a long line of those ... women.

Which made me nice as pie to her. It nearly killed the old bat.

"Hi, Mrs. Kittrick!" I called out the window as I pulled away from the house. "Your yard is gorgeous, as usual!" I waved like we weren't bitter foes and grinned as I looked in the rear-view mirror to see her glaring at my amazing gunmetal gray automotive ass.

That simple act of petty kindness alone eased my anger and brought it down to a non-killing level.

My sisters were enough to make anyone homicidal on a normal day. Add my mom to the mix, and it was a miracle that our house was still standing. Four women who were never, ever wrong was challenging on a good day. The small fact that we'd been here for over one hundred and twenty years didn't help, either.

That whole 'can't die' thing was a pain in my ass. But if we left the area, we lost the immortal factor that had allowed us to live here and threaten one another for over a century. We'd only had one of my sisters leave the Deadwood area, and she'd died over sixty years ago. The rest of us stayed here, fussing and fighting, as my mom said.

As I left the neighborhood, and got out onto the highway, I hit the gas, letting the RPMs vent all my frustration. Normally, my family and I resolved our disagreements easily, being skilled practitioners at the sport, but not this time. This one was too big.

You can't just ignore it when a necromancer moves into your street. You just can't. They have their craft, like everyone else. But their craft involves the dead. That's where they get their power from—the dead. Hence the 'necro' part of necromancer.

Not to mention I'd never met a single necromancer who did his thing for the good of humanity. Nope. They were always self-centered. Usually raging narcissists, and they exploited the dead. Generally, the dead want to be left in peace, but necromancers are based in holding up that process.

So ... no. No ignoring the friendly neighborhood necromancer. Not on my watch.

My mom—known as Meema--didn't agree. She'd been the one throwing the china at me as I left. My sisters, Deirdre and Daniella, didn't feel strongly one way or the other, which was miraculous, but they were tired. We'd had a busy month with a warlock and the tea shop. So they took the path of least resistance.

Which wasn't the path I was advocating. It had escalated from there. Meema wanted to wait and see if he managed to make things troublesome.

I hated to wait and see. This meant that any pets in the neighborhood would disappear suddenly, at the very least. The dead liked to eat when brought back by necromancers. Cats were a favorite. So were nosy dogs.

Not that we had any. But our neighbors did. I didn't even want Mrs. Kittrick's two evil old cats to get eaten. We had a house chicken, but I'd back Evil against a zombie any day of the week.

Three against one meant we were going to wait and see. I didn't understand why we couldn't just go introduce ourselves, and let him know the rules, mainly: One Strike And You're Out.

I shook my head as I blasted down the highway, Bowie wailing from the speakers. This was just making more work for us. We'd have to start a regular patrol of the cemeteries immediately. That was a shit ton of extra work. Keeping the supernatural side of Deadwood, South Dakota on the rails was enough.

As I got closer to the Wyoming border, I realized that this wasn't going to solve my problem. I made a giant loop of a U-turn at the next exit ramp and headed back to Deadwood. But I wasn't going to head home. I'd stop at the Saloon No. 10 and get a Crab Hollandaise burger and a whiskey. Maybe a couple of whiskeys. Comfort food before heading back to face my dragon family.

Not real dragons, or anything like that. Although there were dragons still around. I'd heard of some hiding out down in the Southwest. No dragons in my family. We had enough problems with being witches. Immortality, as long as we never left Deadwood. We could all see ghosts.

And we all had a finely tuned sense of right and wrong. All of us did things to even the playing field, make things square. Meema called it our justice-meter. We also looked out for Deadwood. Granny, long gone, had laid down the law. We protected Deadwood from all the supernatural shit that liked to try and park here and do whatever it was that was on their agenda. It was never anything good for the humans that lived here. Granny had felt coming to Deadwood had not only changed her life but saved it. Looking out for Deadwood was the family business.

Oh, and we had a ghost. A family ghost. Who might even rate higher on the pain-in-the ass scale than my mother and sisters right now.

John Henry Holliday. My grandfather. Yeah, *that* John Henry Holliday.

It was a shame he was already dead. On days like today, I wanted to kill him. This was all John's fault. He and my mother had gotten into it about something—neither would tell us what, which made it worse—and Meema was on a rampage. Another thing that would need to be sorted. There were too many secrets in our house. I shook my head. Later. This would all need to happen later.

Deadwood was quiet today. It was late spring. We had a little more time before the tourists descended en masse on us. Not that I was complaining. I loved the tourists. I didn't know them, and despite the public family business, didn't get to know them. But I loved them nonetheless.

Because it was late spring, Meema closed Monday through Wednesday. I could roll right past our family's tea and herbal shop without feeling any guilt. Thank goddess, because the Crab Hollandaise burger was calling to me in the worst way. I parked and walked in, taking a seat at the bar.

Duffy, the bartender, looked over her shoulder when I sat down. "Hey, Des, what's up?"

I rolled my eyes. "Fighting with Meema and my sisters. What else?"

"Crab?"

"Yes, please." I loved being a local.

Outside of the fact that all I had to do was walk in here, and the bartenders knew what I was having, I loved Deadwood. I wouldn't want to be anywhere else. The fact that who and what I was centered on Deadwood came in second, almost. I truly loved it here.

"What are you drinking?"

"The Stranahan," I said. I loved that they had a good-sized whiskey selection. Even though I didn't stray from my favorites. Right now, it was the Colorado whiskey from the Stranahan down in Denver.

Duffy smiled and poured me a healthy shot, neat. She added a glass of water, and then let me be.

Yeah, it was good to be local.

I stared at the mirrors over the bar, not really seeing them. Someone came in the door, and I felt the breeze from the open door waft over me. Kind of like when you felt ghosts pass by. That was another reason I liked Saloon No. 10. I knew the ghosts here, and they knew me. Actually, a number of them had known me. As the oldest granddaughter of Desdemona Nightingale, saloon and dance hall girl at the Bella Union Saloon, circa 1876, she and my mom, also Desdemona Nightingale, had seen a lot of death. So had I, Desdemona Nightingale number three.

But since we all knew each other, the ghosts here tended to leave me alone unless they were in the mood for a chat. They were terrible gossips. After a hundred years, I was pretty good about ignoring ghosts I didn't want to deal with.

Duffy came out with a plate and set it in front of me. "Here you go, sweets."

"Thanks, Duff." I smiled.

I inhaled the smell of crab and hollandaise. Two of the foods from the goddess. I took a bite and as I was chewing, steps sounded behind me. The proverbial boots-on-hardwood.

"Desdemona Holliday," a deep voice said.

I chewed carefully and swallowed. Then I set my burger down, also carefully. I wiped my hands on my napkin and took a deep breath. I felt the magic gather at my fingers. No one called us Holliday. We were the Nightingales, and the Holliday aspect was kept under wraps.

No exceptions.

I turned my barstool around slowly to see what had to be the brand-new neighbor, since the man in front of me was a necromancer. While he didn't have the normal stink they all seemed to have, he had the look. After a while, you could just tell. He was tall, with dark, longish hair. His face was clean-shaven, and his eyes were the gray-green of a summer storm.

What the hell? Stop it, I told myself. This guy needed to shape up, move, or die. No matter what color his eyes were.

We protected Deadwood. No exceptions.

"I am Desdemona Nightingale. Can I help you?" The magic coiled tightly in my fingers, waiting to be released. One wrong move, pal. Make just one ... and all my aggression is gone for the day. Probably for tomorrow, too.

He frowned. "You call yourselves Nightingale, but we both know the truth."

"Oh? Well, please enlighten me." I swiveled a half-turn and picked up my burger again. "I suppose you can have a seat." I indicated the stool next to me with my burger.

"I did not come here to—"

"I came here for this burger, and I'm not letting it get cold. Sit, or don't." I turned the barstool back to the bar. It was a risk, putting my back to him, but it was better he not suspect anything. Bad enough he knew my real name.

The indecision rolled off him. That was a good sign. At least he didn't plan to off me before I finished the burger. Then he sat down.

"What can I do for you?" I asked.

"I wish to make peace with you."

"I don't understand what you're talking about." The magic waiting in my hands eased in intensity. I didn't know what he wanted, but it seemed there wasn't going to be a showdown at the Saloon No. 10. Which was probably for the best. Damn it.

"I am well aware of what you and your family do here."

My eyebrow went up. I knew it made me seem snotty as hell, but I couldn't help it. "Are you? Then why are you here?"

"My help has been requested."

Oh, this was good. "In what way?" Finishing the burger, I went to work on the fries.

"I would like the chance to help those requesting my ... services without interference from you."

"Really? I'd like all the cats and dogs in our neighborhood to keep on breathing."

"That's not—"

"It's totally realistic and fair, zombie guy," I hissed, leaning closer to him. "And you know it. If you know about my family, then you know better than to come here and try and blow smoke at me."

"We're not all the same."

I laughed. "Yeah, sure. I've met a bunch of you, and yes, you are all the same. It's part of the job description."

He flushed, the color spreading up from his neck into his cheeks. "That's a matter of choice."

"Which totally sells your profession even more, zombie guy."

"I have a name," he grumbled.

"Do I need it?"

"Seeing as we're neighbors, it would be neighborly if you knew it."

"Lay it on me."

"Zane McCallister."

I nodded. "And how long do you plan to stay, Zane McCallister?"

"Depends," he said.

"What can I get you?" Duffy chose this moment to come over, making eyes at me.

Smiling, I gave a little shake with my head. She'd bounce him if I wanted, but I could handle this.

"An iced tea, please." Zane smiled pleasantly at Duffy.

Duffy nodded and moved away.

"Depends on what?" I asked.

"On exactly what my client needs. After that?" He shrugged, making no promises.

"Who is your client? I know most of the dead guys around here."

He gave me a glance that I couldn't interpret. "Yes, I think you probably know this one well."

"Oh?"

"John Holliday."

Damn that man straight to hell.

CHAPTER TWO

I chewed my fries slowly, thinking. I took another bite and when Duffy brought Zane a glass of iced tea, he took it, and busied himself with adding sugar. Okay, he had manners. I'll give him that.

He also smelled good. I could smell him over the fries. He had a clean, outdoors smell—like pine trees. Most necromancers smelled like what we politely called 'grave dirt'. Also known as rotting people. But you know, since we're all polite and mannered here, we'll go with grave dirt.

Zane didn't smell like that. And he wasn't making every fiber of my being want to kill him, damn the witnesses. Was I getting soft?

"I'm sure the fact that John has hired me is a shock to you," Zane said.

"Um, yeah. It is. What is it that he thinks he needs with you?" I struggled to keep my temper under control. I could feel the magic still swirling around my fingers, but I'd stilled it as best I could for the moment. It flared with my temper, and right now, I wanted to blast it all over one John Henry Holliday. But I also wanted to hear just what it was John was up to. So I cooled the magic. For now.

Damn man.

"Well," Zane set his glass down and turned to face me. "He is concerned that he cannot leave. He feels he has been here long enough, and it's not a..." He hesitated. "Pleasant situation," he finished.

"What?" I put the last bite of fries-dipped-in-leftover-Crab Hollandaise bliss into my mouth, and held up a finger. I didn't want Zane McCallister saying another word. I was so mad that John would bring this into our family, and not say anything— wait.

Wait. One. Damn. Minute.

John and Meema had gotten into a rager of a fight today. It made Meema cross as could be, and she'd jumped all over me when I said we needed to just take out the necromancer down the block and be done with it.

Not to mention John and his whatever had totally ruined my meal. The burger couldn't fix everything.

When I'd finished chewing, I said, "Why did you move here?"

An expression I couldn't decipher crossed Zane's face and disappeared. Hmm. That was interesting, and something that would definitely need to be explored. Not right now, however. First things first.

"Because I wanted a new start. I am tired..." He stared down at his glass. "I am tired of the way my life has been going. This seemed like a good place to go to start over."

That made no sense whatsoever. "Do you know—did you know, before you moved here, who we are?" I didn't pretend with other people who were involved in the supernatural world. No sense in being coy. As I wiped my hands on my napkin, I cast a spell around the two of us so anyone within the vicinity would not be able to hear our conversation.

"Of course, I did. Everyone knows that to venture into Deadwood means you have to deal with the Nightingales."

"Then why would you come here?" This still made no sense to me.

He pursed his lips, and I noticed that they were full, and very nice to look at. What the hell?

"I completely understand viewing those who come from outside your town borders as a threat, but you might consider that living somewhere with very active guardians who are unafraid to keep the peace, so to speak, might be an attractive thing?"

I leaned back on the stool. He was right in that I'd never considered it. I always saw supernatural folks who moved in as interested in exploiting the human population. Deadwood, for all its tourist roots, was a small town. It was easy to pick on—or pick off—humans and have no one in the human world the wiser. With Sturgis, we had thousands upon thousands who came here. Some never left. Of those who never left, some met with supernatural occurrences.

So he was right in that I saw most other supernatural folk as a potential threat. This could be a make nice situation where he was trying to butter me up. Not going to happen.

"Really? You're telling me you want to live by a set of rules? Did you flunk necromancer school or something? None of you believe in that sort of thing. You're all glorious individuals. People like me, my family? We're just the mean old sheriffs, dragging you and your art down." I didn't even try to hide the sarcasm in my voice.

"When you live in a state of war, it's hard to see those who are not. But yes, I find the idea of living somewhere with rules and people enforcing them appealing. I'm tired of ... well, that doesn't matter. I didn't come here for any reason other than I thought it would be a good place for me to live as I wish."

"And how is that?"

"Listen, I was planning to come to your home today to speak with you, with all of you. And with John. When I saw you pull off, Tinkie told me—"

"Wait, what? Tinkie told you?" If I wasn't completely mad, Tinkie was one of Mrs. Kittrick's cats. The other one was Winkie. I'd heard her cooing to them.

He flushed. "Yes. I can speak with animals. Tinkie let me know that you'd left in your car, and so I didn't come over."

"What are you?" I asked. This didn't fit with the general description of necromancers.

"I am who I say I am. At this moment, I'm a representative for your grandfather. If you've finished, why don't we go back to your home and speak with the entire family?"

Releasing the spell around us, I gestured to Duffy. "I'll take our check," I said, indicating Zane.

"That's not nece—"

"Be quiet. There's so much going on here. I'm not arguing over a glass of tea with you."

He looked like he wanted to argue, but he only nodded.

I paid the bill and we walked out. I could feel the ghosts gathering around, but they didn't get close, and we were out the door before any one of them could make a play for Zane's attention. Or maybe they'd know what John was up to and had neglected to warn me. I shot them the evil eye as I passed. Traitors. "Where are you parked?" I asked.

"I was walking. I didn't plan on ambushing you at lunch but when I saw your car, I thought it was a fortunate opportunity."

There was something about Zane, about the way he spoke. He was old-fashioned. That was it. He sounded like John did. As though he were from another time, when people spoke slower, more formally.

I sighed. "You can ride back with me. May as well get this over with."

As we got into the car, he smiled briefly, and it made him seem much younger, and very unguarded. "This is a great car."

I wanted to hate this guy, but how do you hate someone who appreciates your baby? "It is. I love it. It was a junker when I found it, and I fixed it and had it painted." Having to be someone else every fifty years or so meant I got a new-to-me fast car. One of the few perks.

We talked cars for the short ride back to Pearl Street. I pulled into the garage. When we got out, I said, "You're on Nightingale ground now. Remember that before you try anything. And also remember, there are four of us."

"I know this. You think I would harm you?"

I shrugged as I walked into the house. "I don't know. I don't know you and can't make any sort of determination as to what you might do. But you've been polite, so I'll return the favor." I led him up the steps to the main level and the huge kitchen, which took up most of the main floor.

Meema was in the kitchen, as was Deirdre. My other sister, Daniella, was working down in the shop. The days we were closed were great for restocking and mixing. Today it was Daniella's turn.

Both Deirdre and Meema turned as we came up. "Are you over your sni—Oh. I didn't realize we had a visitor," Meema said.

Deirdre's eyes met mine, and I nodded. I knew what she was asking. Did we need to be on guard? I could feel the magic swirl and converge around her. I wondered if Zane felt it. As I glanced over at him, he paled just a little under his tan.

Yeah, he felt it. Good.

"We do. This is Zane McCallister. The new neighbor. The new necromancer neighbor, who talks to Tinkie, among other things."

"Why would you talk to that cat?" Deirdre asked.

Zane shrugged. "I was passing by. Tinkie is chatty."

A squawk from the front of the room, where the dining room table sat, caught his attention. We'd opened up the walls between the two rooms when we'd done the renovation.

"What is that?" Zane asked.

"That is Evil," I replied. "He is our house chicken. Given your profession, I would appreciate if you fed any zombies and leave Tinkie, Winkie, and Evil alone."

"Why do you have a house chicken?" Zane asked.

"Stop changing the subject," I snapped, tired of the chitter chatter. "We need to talk."

"Oh, I tried to kill him for supper years ago," Meema answered as though I hadn't spoken. "His head didn't come off, and he ran off, head dangling. We spent a week or so trying to catch him, and he kept evading us. Finally, I gave up. I healed him, and brought him in the house."

"I find it hard to believe you give me any grief about animals at all," Zane said to me. "Attempted dinner to house pet?" He started to laugh.

To my horror, Meema joined him. Deirdre smiled, but she didn't laugh.

"Yes. And we don't feed him to dead people. You need to sit down and tell my mother and sister why it is you are here."

"Would you like something to drink, Zane?" Meema asked.

I glared at her. She was being super friendly to the kind of person we'd been fighting for years. That meant either she was losing her marbles, or she already knew what Zane McCallister was doing here. I kept up the glare, but Meema was a pro at ignoring the building tensions in a room.

"I'm good, thank you." Zane sat at the island, and I sat on the chair on the other end. With Deirdre across from me, even if Meema fell down on the job, we were well placed to deal with anything he might try.

"Tell them," I said.

Zane sighed. "I approached Desdemona today on behalf of

my new client. I will add that I did not seek this client out, but as I met him while walking one afternoon, I decided his request had merit, and agreed to see what I could do to help him. I did not move here for any other reason than the one I told you." He shot me a look. "I like the idea of living somewhere that there are rules, and enforcers. I've lived in places much different before and... well, it doesn't matter. The point is, I didn't seek this case out."

"You're stalling." I crossed my arms.

"I have been hired by your father." Zane nodded at Meema, "And your daughters' grandfather, to help him cross over and leave the mortal world."

Deirdre's mouth fell open. Meema finally lost her hostess-with-the-mostest expression. Her eyes narrowed, and then she looked up at the ceiling. "John Henry Holliday! Get down here!"

There was a silence as we all waited. He might not show up. He and Meema had been yelling, and he was notoriously moody. Finally, he drifted through the stove. "Your dulcet tones reverberated. Am I to assume my company is sought?"

"Yes, it is, you pain in the ass!" I stood up, slapping my hand on the island's butcher block top. "How could you? If you wanted to leave, all you had to do was ask! You didn't need to hire a necromancer! A necromancer? Really?"

John turned to gaze at me. It was amazing how much scorn a ghost could put into a look without a full body behind it. "As my imprisonment here is at the hands of the Nightingale women, I did not assume any of you would be any help."

Meema held up her hand. "You said that earlier, John, and that makes no sense. You can leave any time you like. We have never held you here. Never."

The weight of an anvil landed on my shoulders as the silence stretched out. John finally broke it. "That is decidedly untrue, daughter of mine. I cannot leave."

"What do you mean?" Deirdre asked. "We've never forced you to stay here. I always thought you stayed here because you wanted to."

"Why would I want that?" John shot back.

Deirdre's cheeks went red, a sure sign she was getting mad. "Because we are your family? Is that such a stretch?"

"A family I did not choose, was given no say in, and never knew of while I was alive," John drawled. He leaned, as much as a ghost could, against the stove. I could see him with a cigar hanging out of his mouth, hanging out on the porch of some bar. His accent, while definitely southern, had a western tinge to it. Having grown up here, I knew what people in the west sounded like.

"Jeez, you sound like you hate us," Deirdre said. "That's pretty shitty. What have we ever done to you?"

"You won't let me go!" John shouted. "After Desdemona died, you insisted on keeping me here! I tried to leave, and I couldn't. The grounds of this home had boundaries that I couldn't cross. When you moved the house, I tried to leave again, and you blocked it."

"No, we didn't," I said. "Any barriers we have are to keep certain things *out*. If you're here, and want to leave, you can. We're not stopping you."

"I. Cannot. Leave. The boundaries of the grounds do not allow it," he ground out. If he was in the flesh, his teeth would have been grinding audibly.

"And you couldn't come and talk to us?" I asked. "Why would you go out and hire this guy?"

"Because these are your family grounds. Any magic here is Nightingale magic. I may not have understood magic when I was alive, but over a hundred years with you has allowed me to expand my education. Give me a little credit for being able to figure that out."

"Well, you need some more," I said. "Because we didn't do

this. If you want to go so badly, please do. And why were you and Meema fighting earlier today?" I wouldn't normally air our family business in front of anyone, much less a necromancer, but what the hell? If John had hired Zane, who knew what he'd been spilling. No sense in trying to hide anything now.

That fact pissed me off more than anything else. He'd exposed us through his own selfish, wrong assumptions.

John looked flustered, and Meema crossed her arms as her face closed like a door. Deirdre and I exchanged glances. Something was up here, something more than we realized.

The phone rang. Meema all but leapt to answer it. Saved by the bell, indeed.

"Hello?" she said. She listened, and then gestured at us. "Of course, dear, but why would he—" She stopped, and I could hear the voice of my sister Daniella. She was shouting, although I couldn't make out the words. Meema went very still. "We'll be ready." She hung up.

"Whatever else is going on will need to be tabled," Meema said calmly. "John, I have no issues with continuing this conversation and helping you to whatever end you propose. But we have another matter that insists on immediate attention."

John threw up his hands. "Of course, you do! It's one thing after another with you—"

"That is enough." Meema stopped him in mid-sentence. "Daniella called to let me know that a demon burst into the shop, breaking the lock in the process, and was looking for the Desdemonas. That's what he said." She held up a hand to forestall questions. "She told him none were there, and he said that he'd come and find us. Whatever it is can't be good. I think any other discussions will just have to wait."

"You want to help?" I asked Zane. "Then you need to help us banish the demon." I didn't think we'd need the help. But he was here, and in my eyes, this would be a good test to see what he was really up to.

"Demons aren't really in my job description," he said. "I'm not sure whose job description it is, but it's not pleasant."

I let the magic coil back into my fingers. I was going to blast him on his butt merely for being a candy ass when a loud boom shook the house.

CHAPTER THREE

"Any chance that isn't the demon?" Deirdre asked as we moved to the front door together.

"No chance at all," I replied. Throwing open the door, we cast a silencing spell over Pearl Street. Then I stepped out onto the small porch.

The demon stood in the middle of our one lane road. He was tall, but not ten feet tall, or anything. I'd put him between six and seven feet, the size of the average pro basketball player. He was brown, and it made me think he'd been cooked too long in an oven. He had two sets of horns on his head, and long, scraggly, greasy-looking black hair. The whole effect was topped off with cloven feet and a raggedy loincloth kind of thing that struck me as being on its last legs.

While we stared at him—because goddess, what else could you do?—a car raced up the road. I heard a door slam, and Daniella was pelting toward the house.

"Ward," I yelled, to let her know.

She raised a hand, and I saw an orange spell hit the wards, and then Daniella was within the ward around the house, and she ran to where I stood with Deirdre and Meema.

“Eww,” Daniella said in an aside to Deirdre and me. “I hope that thing stays on.” She nodded to the demon’s sad state of clothing.

Deirdre giggled. “That is something that can’t be unseen.”

“Really, girls.” Meema brushed by us to stand on the edge of the porch. “What do you want?” she called out to Tall, Gross, and Greasy.

“It is good that you are all here,” the demon said in a deep, rumbling voice. ”I have come for the Desdemonas.. “I am owed the souls of two Desdemona Nightingales, and I shall have them. A bargain was made, and it shall be kept.”

Meema smiled as we came up behind her. “Well,” she sounded like she was talking to a customer in the shop. “There has been no bargain made. I am the head of thė Nightingales, and I can assure you none of us has had any dealings with the likes of you.” Her nose wrinkled.

The demon laughed. “Humans, even human witches, are so foolish when puffed up with pride. Stop your yapping, and listen to your betters.”

“Can we just kill him now?” I whispered to Meema.

“I doubt anyone would notice for a while. He doesn’t look like he’s the prom queen or anything,” Daniella added.

Meema held up a hand to quiet us. She said to the demon, “If you have a story to tell, please get on with it. We have other things to do.”

The demon called out in a language none of us understood, and there was a crack in the air. He opened his hand, and there was a rolled piece of parchment in it.

“I’m not getting close to him,” I said.

“Necromancer! I see you hiding among the women,” the demon bellowed. “Come out and bring this agreement to the eldest Desdemona.”

“Oh for hell’s sake,” I said. “I don’t like you, but you don’t have to do that,” I added as Zane pushed past Meema and down the steps. "Well, don't listen to me then. So much for a peaceful life with rules."

Zane walked to the edge of the grass. He held out his hand, and the demon took two steps toward him, and gave him the parchment. Without saying a thing, Zane came back to us. His face was stony as he handed it to Meema. Daniella, Deirdre, and I crowded close to her as she unrolled. A smell rose from the parchment.

"Just gross," I said. "I'm afraid to know where he's been keeping this thing."

"It's flesh," Zane said quietly.

"What?" the four of us said in unison.

"Demons write contracts on the flesh of those they are contracting with."

"What?" Meema's face paled. "This is..." She didn't finish the sentence.

"Human," I said flatly.

"But who?" Deirdre asked. "None of us has been up to anything with this guy."

"Deana?" Meema asked. "I can't see it. She left because she wanted nothing to do with this life." She was referring to our fourth sister, who, like Granny, was long since passed.

"It will be the person who signed it," Zane said.

"Oh, no," Meema said. She staggered into Daniella and me, and Deirdre took the parchment from her. "You need to read it, girls. I don't think I can."

The demon laughed and it was nastier sounding than before. "Truth can be such an unpleasant thing, can it not, ladies?"

"Shut up." I glared at him. "Stop gloating and let us read. You're blowing your wad over there."

"Easy," Zane muttered. "Please."

Deirdre unrolled it again, taking her time.

"Read the contract aloud," the demon commanded. "That way, all shall hear. All shall know."

"Asshole," I whispered.

Deirdre cleared her throat, and then began.

"I, Desdemona Nightingale, do willingly and happily enter into this contract with the demon, Ashlar. The demon Ashlar agrees to meet the terms of my demands. The demands are as follows. First, I shall be gifted with the powers that have lain dormant within my family. I will live always as I am now, until the time comes when I must honor the agreement made between myself and Ashlar. I will secure the life and love I wish for. I am promised a child. This the demon Ashlar grants me." She looked up.

I know my mouth was hanging open. Meema had a hand over her mouth, and I could tell she was trying not to cry. What the hell had Granny given? Were we really not witches, but something from a horrible bargain with this gross thing standing out in the road? My mind struggled to understand. I slammed the door on the struggle. That was not the point right now.

"Go on," Ashlar said.

Deirdre took a breath, stood tall, glared at him and continued reading. "In return for granting what I have asked for, I will surrender the souls of myself and my eldest child when we decide to leave this Earth. We will be called by the demon Ashlar once we shed our mortal bodies, and I agree to answer the call. I come to this agreement of my own will and desire." Deirdre stopped. "Meema, is this Granny's signature?" She handed the parchment over.

Meema accepted the nasty thing back with trembling hands. She looked over it, trailing her hands over the signature at the bottom. "Yes," she whispered. "It's Granny." She sagged against the post of the porch, looking, for the first time since I could remember, like an old woman.

I wanted to curl up and cry. How could Granny do this? What in the ever-loving hell had she been thinking? This was a trap, and there was no way she could get anything out of this. Why had she ever agreed to it? The only person this benefitted was Ashlar. Granny didn't get anything—well, she had, but not for long.

And where in the hell had the demon gotten Granny's flesh from, if what Zane said about contracts was true?

Snatching the parchment from Meema's hand, I stepped off the porch. "Granny—the first Desdemona—has been gone for over a hundred years. And how do we even know this is real? Your kind are not exactly known for being honest."

A rumble of thunder shook the ground beneath me.

"Careful, Desdemona," Zane said. He sounded like he was right behind me, but I wasn't going to turn around and take my eyes off the demon.

"I do not lie. I may not tell the entire truth, 'tis true," Ashlar said. "But I do not lie about agreements. Your grandmother signed that, did she not?"

I didn't answer. I didn't want to. I pressed my lips together tightly.

"That is also the mark of Ashlar," he continued. "We made an agreement, and it was done willingly by Desdemona Nightingale. I delivered the things I promised. The weak human love she wished for—was he not with her until her death?"

"I don't think that was the way she wanted it," I shot back. "A ghost is not a substitute for a man."

Ashlar shrugged. "That is not my concern. She made her request, and I granted it. She had all the powers of the Nightingale women, did she not? She—" He stopped, and grinned. "And do you, her offspring, not share in those powers?"

He'd been about to say something else. I could tell. He wasn't lying, but he sure wasn't telling us everything. And that contract! What a piece of crap that was! Why would Granny have signed it? For John? For a man? I just didn't buy it. There was more, and Ashlar knew it.

But he wasn't telling. I narrowed my eyes as I shot my best glare at him, trying to will him to continue speaking.

"This was not the life she wished for," Meema said. She sounded stronger, and she joined me on the lawn.

Deirdre came to stand on my other side with Daniella. "Your bargain was with our grandmother. She isn't here. The fact that you believe she did not honor the agreement is not on us."

The demon took a step closer, putting one hoof onto the lawn. "But it is, Nightingale daughter. You see, your grandmother cheated. She pretended to honor the agreement."

"That doesn't sound like Granny," I objected. I felt a hand on my shoulder. I knew it was Zane, and I felt the warning in his touch. I could feel his concern and his fear.

Ashlar continued as though I hadn't spoken. "When you turned eighteen, daughter of Desdemona, I came for her, and for you. She waited for me, on the same porch where you stand now. She said that she would be out within an hour, and she wanted the time to prepare the things that had to be done. I care naught for the concerns of humans, but I prefer the souls to come with as little as struggle as possible. I granted her an hour, and at the appointed time, returned to claim my souls. The women—the supposed Desdemonas—were sitting together on the porch, and I called out to her. She raised her head, and said, 'We have been ill. But we are here to honor our bargain.' Her head fell forward, and she stopped speaking. The women were very close to death. Which does not matter to me. I gathered the souls, and I left, believing that the human woman had honored that which she promised."

He looked up, and for a moment, made me think of an impatient businessman. Then he glared at all of us, and it was like the fires of hell opened up from his gaze. "Imagine my surprise when recently, the younger of the two souls informed me that she was not, in fact, Desdemona. That Desdemona had bought their lives. She took care of the children that would be orphaned—for this woman and her mother both had a wasting sickness, and both were dying. There were a number of humans that would suffer their loss." Ashlar waved a hand, dismissing children losing a mother as an aside.

I hated him for that. And there hadn't been anything in the contract about a specific date. Which was Granny's mistake. You didn't leave demons wiggle room. They always wiggled, and the human ended up screwed. Why ask for immortality if you and your kid only had eighteen years? It didn't make sense.

But that was the hell of wiggle room in contracts. Those who put it in a contract were planning to use the wiggle room before the ink dried.

"In return, they agreed to let me take them. The woman informed me they'd already lived through hell on Earth, so the possibility of Hell did not frighten them. She and her mother lasted a long time in my realm," he added. "They were fighters. The younger of the two spilled all she knew at the end, otherwise I'd have no knowledge of these trivial details. I know you humans prize them, however."

What had he done to them? I didn't think you could destroy a soul, but he spoke of them as in the past. Why was he telling us all this? It didn't make any sense.

"All of which matters not. The agreement has not been fulfilled. I will have the two Desdemonas that were promised."

"Are we sure the first Desdemona isn't already in Hell?" Zane asked behind us in an undertone.

All four of us turned to glower at him. "You really want to die right now? I could fit it in, despite the crowded schedule," I said.

"That's if you beat me to it," Deirdre said.

"We do not agree to this." Meema dismissed Zane with a look that would have killed him had she been focused. "I will not be party to a bargain I had no hand in."

"No matter," Ashlar said. "You were made party by one who had the right to speak for you."

"Not for my soul," Meema countered.

"I have been patient. I have allowed for explanation when none was required. You will come with me now and attempt to make amends for the betrayal of your mother." Ashlar crossed his arms, manifesting extreme boredom. "This discussion is over."

"The silencing spell is slipping," Zane said.

"Then be useful and shore it up!" Meema snapped. "Girls," she said.

We knew the tone. It was our word, our way of making ready.

"Love you," Meema, Deirdre, Daniella and I said together.

Meema had insisted. She said we never knew what might happen, and you always wanted to tell your loved ones how you felt.

As one, we sent a vanquishing spell toward Ashlar. It shot out of our hands, varying shades of green.

Our action took Ashlar by surprise. The spell hit him as he moved. It exploded in a shower of green stars against his leg.

"Betraying witches!" he screamed. "You will all suffer! *Kaabe't'aek shu'eshak!*"

"Oh shit," Zane yelled. Obviously he understood what the hell Ashlar had just said. "*Peregrinatione ad angustos*!"

"You asshole!" I screamed. "You're not getting my soul or anyone else's!" Ashlar had cast a soul calling spell. I could tell by Zane's response. It wouldn't just hit us, but everyone around.

And we protected Deadwood. No exceptions.

At least the necromancer was helping. "*Peregrinatione ad angustos!*" I shouted as a red light flew from my hands. Meema and Deirdre joined me, and we cast the spell wide. I didn't want anyone in Deadwood to pay the price for our family baggage.

The demon roared, and threw back his head and opened his mouth. Flame shot out, and when he lowered his head, the flame came toward us. It scorched and killed anything living it touched. The grass and the rosebushes were blasted into bits of ash. But nothing else seemed to catch fire.

"*Daemon ignis*," Zane shouted. "Duck! *Praefundo*!"

The four of us dropped to the ground. A torrential rain poured down on it. It wasn't just water—it was ice cold, and it extinguished the fire.

Demon fire. Ashlar was pissed. I'd read about it but never seen it before. Everything I'd read said demons don't pull this out a lot because it makes them...it makes them weak.

"*Victa*," I whispered to Deirdre.

She nodded and whispered to Meema and Daniella.

"On three," I said. "One, two, THREE!" I shouted the last word.

Meema, Daniella, Deirdre and I stood up, clasping our hands together, and thrusting them to where Ashlar stood. "*Victa*!" we shouted.

I put everything I had into it. Ashlar screamed, a bone-crushing scream I'd never heard before. It made my head hurt, and my ears were wet, as though they were bleeding. I felt tears come from my eyes, and my nose was running.

I glanced over at Meema and my sisters to see how they were holding up.

They *were* bleeding. Eyes. Ears. Nose. Oh my God. He was going to make us bleed to death.

Vaguely, as from far away, I heard someone shout, "*Praesidio*!"

A coolness came over me, and a rush of liquid from my ears. Everything was so much quieter now. The scream that had hurt so much when I'd first heard it was fading. I was still holding Deirdre's hand, but she seemed far away, too.

It was all getting better. I could see Ashlar, but he was fading. There was a light where he stood, and all around him was dark. Black. The blackness closed in, making the light around him smaller and smaller until he was merely a blurred image within a tiny sun.

Something tugged at me, but I couldn't turn my head. I couldn't keep my eyes open. What was I doing? I was saying something. Doing something. But … whatever it was moved away, far away. And I couldn't be bothered to look for it, or discover what it might have been.

I needed to close my eyes. A jerk on me, on my arm, and then blessed darkness.

Love you, I thought. *Love you*. The darkness went over my head, and carried me further under, and I gave myself up.

CHAPTER FOUR

My feet hurt. Not just tired feet, but like they were burning. Like, hanging out in a fireplace burning. I tried to open my eyes, but my eyelids were shut, and that feeling when you get up, and your eyes are crusty? That was it, but on crack.

"Jesus," I whispered.

"He is not here. Much as it might do him good," a deep voice rumbled in front of me. At least, it sounded like it was in front of me.

"Where am I?" I muttered. I was late for something, I'd been too late—what was it? I couldn't remember, and my feet hurt, and my damn eyes were itching and horrible. I shook my head, and remembered that I had an arm.

It weighed a ton, but I was able to clumsily drag it across my eyes. Painfully, I opened them, and forgot how to breathe.

The scene before me was awful. Dark, with red tints. There was movement all around. Everywhere my hurting eyes could see, there was movement, roiling and rolling and slithering. All of it was interspersed with pain. Pain so deep that it made me hurt to see it. Everywhere, darkness and movement and pain. There was nothing else. No light. No space. Nothing but pain.

"Beautiful isn't it?"

I turned my head to see a brown creature—a demon—next to me. I knew him. I should know him. His name. His name was ... Ashlar.

Oh my goddess. Everything came back to me in a rush, and I fell back against whatever I was leaning on, shaking with the memory.

"Ah. Good. You remember. Sometimes, it takes people a while to come to their past. The shock of coming here is overwhelming for some. I do have to say that I am pleased with you, Desdemona Nightingale. You came back to yourself in a matter of moments. The blink of an eye, as you humans say." He found this amusing, and laughed uproariously at his own wit.

"Asshole," I said.

"Even better. You are still yourself. It will make our time together more fulfilling. Perhaps I shall be mollified." He tapped his finger against his lips. Then he looked at me. "But I doubt it. I am a vengeful creature, and your family is indebted to me."

"Don't ... owe you ... shit," I ground out. It hurt to speak. It even hurt to breathe, but I had to keep doing that. At least, I think I did. I'd never been to Hell before. Maybe the rules were different.

"Gaze upon it," he said, like we were discussing the weather. "There it is. One of the most beautiful sights in Hell."

Apparently I didn't gaze appreciatively enough at the green goo floating above us because he spat at the ground in disgust. "You humans. Everything about you is small. You think small. You live small. And you die small. Your mother, who was promised to me? She is doing her small, human bit. She is up there."

I looked up again, frantic to see Meema. I didn't think she

was here. I thought I was here alone. I followed where his clawed hand pointed. As I stared, details became clearer. What I thought was green goo was moving, and within whatever it was were ... people. I gasped.

"Yes, that is the River of Souls. When a soul comes to Hell, that is their final resting place. They are moved on the whims of Hell. They have no control, no input in their being. They just are. And they are aware of it all," he added with great relish.

"Your mother is there. She is living out her final days, the rest of her days, as a small piece of the River of Souls. Like so many other humans, she is only useful in being a part of something bigger." His voice was malicious. "Unlike you, she did not survive the journey. Or she would have been here next to you. It's a pity, but at least not a complete waste."

I will not cry. I will not, I thought. Not in front of this asshole. I knew he was taunting me, wanting to get a rise out of me. That's how demons are. They enjoy hurting, and causing pain.

Which is why the thought of Granny making a bargain with this douchebag was as painful as anything else that was happening to me. I finally glanced down at my feet. They were not on fire, but they itched and burned terribly. I wanted to scratch them and never stop, but I couldn't move.

"You feel it, do you not?" His voice was close to my ear, whispering, filled with glee. "The fires of Hell? It's different, I am told, when one is actually dead. When a human is brought to Hell, in their human form, the very auspices of Hell rebel against it. This is a place for demons, for the fallen, and for souls that belong here. Humans were never meant to be here, much as some of you deserve it. So when you are here, your being, and the powers of Hell know there is something wrong. I will keep you human, third Desdemona, until your human form fails. Once that happens, your soul will still be here, still be mine." He laughed. "Life has been rather boring. This will bring some excitement into it. Once I have your soul, I will find the next Desdemona."

"There isn't another one. I'm the last."

"Is that so? There are other Nightingales. One by one, I shall have them."

"You have me and Mee— my mother. That's what you said you wanted!"

He laughed. "It was. But when a bargain agreed upon is not fulfilled, I am no longer bound to my agreement. Thus, I have decided that I will have all the Nightingales."

"That's not what you said!" I whisper-shouted. It hurt too much to speak louder.

"I did not share everything with you in the moment, no." Seeing my look of fury, he laughed some more. "I always win. No matter what you humans try, I always win. You will not be lonely for too long."

Smiling, with his hands on his hips, he turned away from me. "Get in here!" he bellowed.

There was silence, and then a scurrying of limbs, along with small whimpers. What fresh hell was this? As I watched, my feet still itching, and tears leaking from my eyes, an assortment of creatures hurried in. I couldn't see any one creature. They moved en masse, bowing and scraping. The fear from them was a palpable stench.

There was a lot of weird hair, and odd colors, and claws, but I felt pity. These creatures were consigned here as much as I was, and they were afraid of this asshole. The way the fear was coming off them, they lived in fear. The fear had come into the room before they did. And Ashlar stood there grinning like a proud parent.

He really needed to die. I put that on my To-Do list. Once I got out of here, his ass was mine.

"Watch her. She does not sleep. She does not move. She does not do anything other than stay awake and observe. If you see that she is beginning to move about, you are to immobilize her. Is that understood?" Ashlar asked.

The herd of little demons all nodded and bowed and made assenting noises. "I will return, and I expect her suffering to have increased. Take it in turns. She is never to be alone." Ashlar stared down at me. "There, you see? I am an attentive host. I shall return." He walked away from me and then disappeared.

All the small demons looked at me with wide eyes. They began speaking among themselves. Whatever they were saying, I couldn't understand it. But whatever it was escalated, and they were rolling around on the floor, shouting, kicking, biting.

When the dust—helldust?—settled, one small demon, with a long nose, big eyes, and arms that hung to the floor was left. The other demons hurried away, and it was just me and the little guy. Like everything else here, he radiated suffering. Sadly, he waved his hand at me.

I felt my body press down against whatever I was lying on.

I had to get out of here. But how? I'm generally an optimist, but things were looking rather bleak. If I did nothing, I would die here. Not for a long time, according to Ashlar the Tour Guide, but I would die. I would never see my family again.

At the thought of my mother, tears fell down my cheeks. They dried up before they reached my jaw, and the salt in the tears made my face itch. Everything itched. My feet were still the worst. A shuffling noise next to me made me turn my head—slowly—and see what the little misery demon was doing.

His eyes, if it was possible, were bigger. If I didn't know better, I'd say he was about to burst into tears.

"What's next on the agenda?" I got out. Wiggling my upper body allowed me to scratch my back and ease some of the itching.

His eyes widened, and he said, "Beeval."

"What? I don't speak Hell." I didn't even know if there was a Hell language.

He peered around, his movements fearful. Then he crept closer, laid one long-fingered claw on my hand, and pet it like you'd pet a cat. "Beeval," he said. He looked directly at me, and used the other hand to point to himself. "Beeval."

"Your name is Beeval?" I asked.

The corners of his mouth turned up, and he got all watery-eyed again. "Beeval, Beeval," he repeated.

"Desdemona," I said. "I'm Desdemona."

"Desimo?" Beeval sounded it out slowly.

"Close enough. Beeval, can you help me?" I tried to sit up, but I was bound to this board, or whatever I was lying on. The hospitality around here sucked.

His hand slid off mine and he took a couple of steps back. His hands flew to his mouth, and he shook his head violently.

"Beeval, do you like Ashlar?"

Beeval clamped his hands on his mouth, his eyes wide over the top of them. Slowly, he shook his head again, but much less violently.

Jeez. This guy Ashlar was a douche to everyone. This guy, or mini-demon, or whatever he was—he wasn't much taller than my chicken Evil. He was also scared to death.

"Beeval, if you help me get out of here, I will take you with me."

"With you?" His lip trembled.

I nodded. The small action made every part of my body hurt, and I wanted to scream out. I ground my teeth and stifled my scream. This was my only chance, my only hope.

Beeval scanned the room once more, obviously frightened, and turned and ran off.

Shit. That was my only hope, and it had hightailed away from me. My head fell back against the whatever it was I was on, and I let my body sag into it. I was not going to get out of here. My mother was gone. I stopped that train of thought. I couldn't afford to get on that right now. I'd be a hopeless, quivering mess.

Shuffling from the tunnel where Beeval had run off to caught my attention. Beeval came through it breathing heavily. "You go," he said.

"I want to, but I can't." I strained my arms and legs to show him I was magically bound.

Beeval snapped his fingers, and I fell off the table/board/whatever.

"Holy hell!" I swore softly, hissing with the pain. The itching that my being here brought on was now given the pain cherry on top by having a burning sensation where my body touched anything of Hell. "This place is one big social disease," I muttered.

"Hurry," Beeval said. "We hurry." He came over next to me and tugged on one of my hands. "Hurry," he said again, and I could hear the fear in his voice.

I scrabbled to my feet, wincing at how much this hurt. Beeval clamped onto my arm and dragged me along. Instead of the tunnel he'd just come through, he led us off to the right, and there was a faint line in the wall. He wiggled his claws, and the line began to glow. After about ten seconds, the glow was gone, and Beeval pushed the wall. A small door opened.

"Here. This take you out."

I crouched down, feeling all of my hundred plus years old. "You go first. We go together."

"No, no! You go, I follow." He moved behind me and pushed my back. "Go now. Go now."

"All right, but you follow me," I said. I got onto all fours, and stuck my head in. I barely fit. Good thing I kept it low key with the Saloon 10 burgers. It was a tight squeeze. "Hey, what am I looking for?"

He ducked down near my foot. “There is opening. You push through. Take you home.”

“Okay. Keep up, Beeval.” I couldn’t see around me very well. I had to look down and behind me between my legs. Completely uncomfortable.

I felt his claws pushing at my feet and I started to crawl. For all that Hell was making me miserable, it sure didn’t want to let me go. It felt like the tunnel was closing in. I yelped when something cut into my left arm. From my shoulder to my wrist, a searing pain made me bite my lip so hard it bled.

“I am going to kill Ashlar. I’m going to kill him.” I tried to check things out behind me but I couldn’t tell if Beeval was there. “Beeval?”

Nothing. Shit. Was this a trap? Everything felt off-kilter. I couldn’t tell. If I was going to die, I might as well do it balls to the wall. I’d count Beeval as an ally until he gave me a reason not to.

“Beeval, keep up, please! I don’t want to lose you.” The red light behind me dimmed, making the tunnel darker and closer. My hair caught on things I didn’t even want to try and imagine, and yanking the hair free made tears come to my eyes.

Smoke began to fill around me. “Oh, for Pete’s sake!” I screamed, and stopped when the acrid smell hit me, making me choke. My hands went to my neck, and I coughed and coughed. I put my head down and tried to cover my mouth and nose with my shirt, which didn’t seem to be in good shape.

Finally, it cleared, and eyes watering and throat burning, I started crawling again. I could feel things catching against my arms. When I made it out of here, I would be a mess. Which was putting it nicely.

My head bumped into something. I fell back a little and peered in front of me. It was blocked. “What the hell?” I yelled. Had Beeval tricked me? Was this a trap? Where was he? I bent my head down and peered into the darkness behind me. He wasn't there.

It *was* a trap. Ashlar had cooked this up to make me think I was getting out here. "No," I whispered. "I will not stay here."

How long I sat there, crouched on all fours, trying to figure a way out, I didn't know. I wanted to use magic, but I was afraid to draw any attention to myself. Magic calls to magic. If I used my magic, Ashlar would find me and drag me back. I pushed on the dirt and rock in front of me, but it didn't move. Still, I kept pushing, scrabbling with my fingers, getting a rock free and using it like a shovel, anything. Sweat ran down every part of me and the rock slipped from my hands as I tore off a nail.

"Damn it!" I yelled. I pushed at the rock and dirt barrier once more, and then banged my head as I flew backward. Well, as much as you can fly backward with six inches to spare all around you. My hands burned as flame shot out of them.

I'd never done that before. The flames were so bright I had to cover my eyes—it wasn't the flames. The flames, flames that I'd shot out of my hands, like a dragon or something, had broken through the barrier and the light I was seeing was from my place. Earth. It wasn't the glow of Hell. It was moonlight, shining so pure and bright above me that it made my eyes hurt.

I pulled the rest of the barrier apart, hardly knowing what I was doing, until I was able to squeeze through. I fell onto the ground crying. I'd made it.

"Beeval!" I sat up. The hole was still there, although it looked weird. "Beeval!" I shouted as loud as I dared. There was no answer, and I didn't expect it. Somewhere along the way, he'd disappeared, if he even followed me at all. I didn't know if he was a good guy, or a bad guy that had set out to trap me, and I'd beaten it—but he'd saved my life.

As I watched, the hole shimmered, and shrank. I couldn't stop staring as it covered itself over. "I'm so sorry, Beeval." I cried some more. The pain and suffering that was visible on him hadn't been fake. I knew that. He'd risked himself to get me out.

Ashlar had to die.

But first, I needed to get home and get a shower. And some burn cream. And probably another shower. Maybe even a third. I got up. "Time to get your ass in gear," I muttered.

CHAPTER FIVE

I fell back onto the grass. Never before had I been so grateful to lie in the grass. Even though I really needed to be up and moving, this felt like the best thing I'd ever experienced. It was about a thousand degrees cooler, and as my body adjusted to not being slow cooked, all the things that hurt in me began to make themselves known. I lifted an arm and cast a soothing spell over myself. I didn't have time to fool with this now. When I got home, Meema and my sist—my thought stopped. Meema would never be there again. There would only be the three of us. Deana, our fourth sister, had died, and even though I hadn't seen her much after she ran off to Los Angeles, I missed her. She wrote, and kept us up to date with all that happened. When she passed away, her daughter, also Deana, took over the letter writing. They still had three generations going: niece, grandniece, and great grandniece. But in Deadwood, it would be just us.

The first and the last.

Okay. Enough of the pity party. Yes, things were depressing at the thought of Meema being gone. Moping wouldn't get me home, or kill Ashlar. And those were the priorities, in that order. I stood up, and staggered.

I needed to cast some sort of concealment spell over myself. If I saw me walking by, I'd call the cops. I had to look terrible, given the way I felt. With a shaking hand, I cast one, and straightened. I had to figure out where I'd come out of Hell into.

This wasn't Deadwood. Crazy as it sounds, I could tell. Our magic was tied to Deadwood. Must have been part of the deal that Ashlar made with Granny, yet another part that he didn't bother to tell her. Jerk. When we left it, our magic disappeared. We became fully human and lost our immortality.

I couldn't make shoes appear, sadly, so slowly, carefully, I made my way toward the road. Once I figured out where I was, I needed to make a note of this place. So that we'd always know there was a tunnel that opened up here from Hell from their side.

Squinting up at the moon with eyes that were still sensitive, I noted that it was full. Funny. It wasn't supposed to be full for another four days when I left. Which meant I'd been gone at least four days. Or a month and four days. I wouldn't know until I made it home.

There wasn't a lot of traffic here. I needed to find a main road. You'd think, in this day and age, it wouldn't be a big deal to get around. But when you have no phone, no money, and no shoes, it might as well be the wild west. Looking around, I stopped and gasped.

I was in the Mt. Rushmore National Memorial. That meant I was an hour from home. I could be home in a couple of hours.

If I could find a ride. I was so tired, I didn't know how long or how well my concealment spell would hold up. It didn't matter. This had to work. There was no other choice. A ranger station might be my best bet. The memorial was to my right, so I needed to walk away from it. That's where most of the tourist stuff was. Everywhere had been built to make sure you could see the memorial. I did almost a one-eighty and I could see the amphitheater and all the buildings. Oh, please, let there be a night guard or something.

Limping along, I marveled at how quiet, how peaceful it was at night. I couldn't believe there was a tunnel to Hell here.

Shock, or something else overtook me. It was a thought I was reborn, and it wasn't better. Reborn out of Hell. Hell born. I started to giggle. This meant I needed to sit down, drink some tea, and get taken care of. I was on the edge of falling apart.

As I walked down the stone-lined path, I saw a building off to the side that said 'Ranger Station' on the side of it. There was a light on. I blinked a few times, adjusting my eyes to the light. I thought they were all right. But this was great. I didn't want to break into the place if I could avoid it. I pulled open the door.

"Hello?" I called.

The squeak of chair wheels on the floor came from behind a wall, followed by footsteps. An older man, with graying hair and a park ranger's uniform, came out, his mouth dropping open when he saw me.

"Can I help you miss? What in God's name happened to you?"

I laughed at little at his phrase. God had nothing to do with this. "I got into a fight and lost."

"With what? A bear?"

"No, sir, with a douchebag of guy. Would it be possible to use your phone?"

"If you call an ambulance."

"I'm from Deadwood. If I can make a call to my sisters, they'll come get me and we'll go right to the hospital."

He was inspecting me. My concealment spell must not have been holding up well. "Yeah, I think you'd better put that first on your list. Where is the guy? How did you get in the park?"

I sighed, readying myself to lie when he held up a hand.

"Don't answer that. Let's get your family called, and then you can tell me about it. We'll call the police. Come on back."

"Could I get some water, please?" My throat was so dry, from Hell, from the dust, from the screaming, everything.

"Course you can. What's your name?"

"Desdemona. Desdemona Nightingale."

That made him stop. "That's a beautiful name. Hey, are you related to Nightingale's Tea and Herbs?"

"That's my shop, well, my family's shop." I dropped into a chair in front of what I hoped was his desk.

"My wife loves your tea. Won't buy it anywhere else."

I smiled. "What's her name?"

"Julia Ann. Julia Ann Harwood. I'm Wil Harwood," he added. "Here, use my phone." He slid the office phone to me and I slowly dialed the house number.

"Hello?" Daniella answered.

"Dani, it's me," I said quietly.

"Oh my stars! Desi! Where are you? Are you all right?"

"No, I've had an awful day. Ashlar beat the heck out of me, and I only made it away from him. I'm over at Mt Rushmore. Can you come and get me?"

Another thing Meema taught us? Give the pertinent information, and don't gush or carry on. There would be time for that later. Do what needs doing first, then take the time to sort it all out. It saved a lot of time and questions when action was called for.

"We're leaving now. Where do we go?"

"Where should I have them meet me?" I asked Wil. I'd have to tell him some more than I had. He was listening to the conversation carefully.

"Have them meet us right at the parking lot. You can stay here until they get here."

Oh, yeah. He was going to grill me. "Meet us at the parking lot. I'm in a ranger station, and the ranger will let me stay here until you get here."

"We're on the way. Love you," she said. She didn't ask about Meema.

I was profoundly grateful. I'd avoided thinking about her because when I did, I saw the green floating goo above me, and all those souls within it. Undoubtedly, some of them deserved Hell. But how many were like me and Meema, brought there against our will? Ashlar hadn't sounded like this was his first rodeo.

"Love you, too." I'd have to tell her, tell them both. And I didn't want to. I didn't want to see the River of Souls. Not even in my memory. That's not how I wanted to remember Meema.

Daniella hung up. I knew she'd be in the car within minutes. I hung up and leaned back in the chair, preparing myself. Wil brought me a bottle of water, and then sat down across from me.

I didn't usually use magic on others. It felt like taking advantage of them, and created potential problems. You always saw stories about how the supernatural creatures, whatever they were, erased the memories of humans as they needed to. It didn't work that way. The brain is a funny thing. It wants to remember, as long as the situation isn't too awful.

Wil would remember this. It was better to make him think I'd had a fight with a boyfriend, or something like that, and then distract him. He'd remember me as a nice lady with crap taste in guys, but nothing to get excited about.

"What's Julia Ann's favorite tea?"

He smiled. "She loves a lot of the black tea and fruit mixes."

I nodded. "Tell her to come in and see me in a couple of weeks. I'll blend her something and call it the Julia Ann."

Will threaded his fingers together and gazed at me. "You don't have to do that."

"I know I don't. But you literally saved my life, Wil. I woke up, face down in the dirt, and I didn't know where I was.

Once I looked around, I figured it out. I didn't think anyone would be here, but you are. Thanks to you, I'll be able to get home."

"You going to report this to the police?"

Here we were, the crux of the matter, as far as Wil Harwood was concerned.

"I don't know. I need to get checked out, and I need to take some time to feel better."

"Ashlar the name of the guy who hurt you?"

I didn't think he could summon the demon merely by using his name. It was better to be safe than sorry. "That's what he calls himself. His real name is Gerald Reid."

"Gerald Reid?"

I forced a laugh. "Yes. Ashlar is his stage name."

"What kind of stage?"

"He has a band."

Wil nodded. Sadly, that was all I needed to say. Since I had long, unruly hair, and a nose ring, and my burns looked like, I hoped anyway, tattoos, all began to make sense in his world. A guy with more dream than talent, and the poor girl who had gotten caught up with him.

This was far better than using magic. People see what they want to see. If you show them what they expect, you and your situation become normal, and nothing to make a fuss about. I was all about not making any sort of fuss.

We chatted for the next hour about tea, and Deadwood, and tourists, interspersed with Wil's offers to get the first aid kit. Since I wasn't bleeding to death, I declined. I had no idea what to do with a Hell burn, but no human first aid kid would even touch it.

Wil's phone rang, and when he answered it, he glanced at me and gave a thumbs up. "They're out front. Come on, I'll drive you over. You look dead on your feet."

I nodded and took his arm when he offered it to me. He

helped me into a golf cart and sped off to the entrance. When he unlocked the gate, I saw Daniella's Jeep . "That's my sister."

He helped me out of the cart and walked me over to her car. Deirdre got out of the passenger seat and put her arms around me carefully. "We didn't think we'd see you again." She pulled away, and she was crying.

"Desdemona tells me that you're going to the hospital straight away."

"We are," Daniella said from the driver's side.

Deirdre got into the back, and I lifted myself into the passenger seat. "Thank you," I said across the Jeep out the window on the driver's side. "Have Julia Ann come into the shop. I mean that."

"I will. And you call me and let me know that you're doing all right. And I mean that, young lady."

"Yes, sir," I said, smiling. It felt good to be here, with my sisters. They helped to begin righting the world around me.

Daniella waved and made a U-turn, and we headed back to Deadwood. For the first time since we'd fought Ashlar, I relaxed. I sank into the seat and closed my eyes. When I opened them again, Daniella was pulling up in front of the house. She got out and helped me out. Since I'd been sitting for over two hours, all my muscles were stiff and sore.

"We need to treat all those burns," she said.

"Were you able to conceal them?" Deirdre asked behind us.

"Yes. I dropped the spell once I was in the car."

"How do you feel?" Deirdre asked.

She wasn't being trite. Magical wounds worked differently, and sometimes would have an effect long after the wound was inflicted.

"Like someone ran me over, and then tried to set me on fire." There was so much to tell them. "Do you think I can shower soon?"

Daniella led me into the kitchen. "Let us look at all this, and see what we can do, and then yes, you can shower. But I think this might take more than one session of healing."

I sank into one of the kitchen chairs. "I figured that. I'm just glad I'm here."

They exchanged glances, and I saw all the questions, but they tabled them as they sent healing spells to me for various aspects. The burns weren't going to go away. I knew the damn Hell burns would be different. I'd just have to tell people I'd gone on a tattoo bender. That they were tribal.

I closed my eyes and let my sisters work.

CHAPTER SIX

After they healed as much as they could, I staggered up the stairs to my room, declining any help. I stayed in the shower until the water ran cold, and when I got out, I wrapped what was left of me in a robe, and my hair in a towel, and fell into bed.

When I woke, it was morning. I didn't want to move. Meema was gone. Once I got up, that was it. It was a new day here on Pearl Street, and we'd have to go on without her. There'd be no pretending otherwise. I lay in bed for a little while longer, pretending the old life was here.

Now that I was home, in the home we'd shared, the loss of her hit me hard. She would never make me crepes again. That was one of her comfort foods when we'd had a hard time—a crepe of our choice. We all knew how to make them, but they would never be Meema's crepes ever again. Today would have been a perfect crepes kind of day.

I curled onto my side and cried for a while. I needed to get this out, so that I could tell my sisters without completely breaking down. I didn't know if I'd be successful, but I had to try.

Granny had died when we were nine. Meema took over all the things that Granny had done. None of us realized it at the time, but she handled a lot. And she'd been handling it for over one hundred years. When we were twenty, Meema had told Deana to go, to seek what she wanted, and kissed her and saw her off with love. Somehow, Meema had known. Deana didn't leave for a couple of months, and she snuck away. But Meema had saved every one of Deana's letters, and gone to visit her grave in Los Angeles.

How in the hell were we going to survive without her? It was only a couple of days ago I was complaining that we were fighting again. She'd thrown a plate at me.

Stalling wasn't going to make this better. I needed to share all that had happened, and we needed to figure out how to kick the shit out of Ashlar before I stabbed him in his greasy black heart. And I needed to find out what had happened to Beeval. I couldn't get the little demon out of my mind. I hoped he was still alive and in one piece.

Given who his boss was, who knew what had happened to him? I couldn't let the issue of what happened to him rest. Maybe the necromancer would be some help here.

It was time to get up. So that's what I did--I got up and got dressed, and did the next thing I was dreading. I looked in the mirror. The woman who looked back at me wasn't the same woman I'd seen the last time I'd left the house.

My hair, usually dark, had red highlights. No bald spots that I could see or feel. That was some kind of miracle. My burns were the worst. On my arms, it looked like I'd been run over by something. There was one on my neck, and another on my chest that I couldn't figure out. Oh, wait. I'd choked and grabbed at my neck. When I inspected the burns on my neck and chest carefully, I could see my handprints.

Weird. I wondered why my handprints would burn me. Another thing I had Hell to thank for. And that bastard Ashlar.

I was going to kill him if it was the very last thing I ever did. Even if I ended up in the River of Souls. I probably would get my chance soon. I didn't think my absence would go unnoticed. Even though it seemed sort of pointless, I sent out a prayer to anyone who might be listening that Ashlar was lazy and inattentive to his prisoners, and that I'd have a week or so before he came back.

Dressed in jeans, boots, and a plain grey T-shirt, I went downstairs. I could hear people talking in the kitchen. God, we still had to deal with the concern of what to do with our resident ghost, who hadn't been seen since Ashlar showed up.

When I walked into the kitchen, Deirdre was at the stove, and Daniella sat at the bar. Zane, the necromancer-who-wouldn't-go-away, sat next to her, and John Holliday, Resident Ghost, leaned against the other end of the island.

Evil was inside, and when he saw me, he chicken-walked over to me and pecked my shoe. I leaned down to pet him. Ever since Meema healed him, he was more than a normal chicken. He wasn't even the sort of chicken that was good for eating. A customer had given Meema eggs years ago, and this one had hatched. He was, we discovered later, along with all the other eggs, a blue-silver Sumatran chicken, best for those wanting a pet. He was a streaky black and white on top with a gorgeous, green shiny body and huge tail.

Meema had no interest in a pet at that time. Sumatrans, we learned afterwards, were not good layers. Meema figured that out pretty quick. After he matured, and he didn't show much interest in the hens, which was the only reason to keep a rooster, she decided that skinny or no, he was headed for the pot. Plus, he had the most gorgeous tail feathers. But when she'd gone to lop off his head, she didn't get a clean shot. He leapt off the chopping block, and Meema spent the next week trying to catch the rooster with the half-lopped off head. She gave up finally, and used magic to heal him.

He'd been an inside bird since then. We'd stopped keeping chickens years ago. Evil was close to thirty years old, and showed no signs of slowing down. Meema said she must have given him a little more juice than she'd planned.

I stroked his head again. He pecked at my boot top, and wandered away.

"How are you doing?"

"Well, I need to come up with some amazing tattoo stories. If I've got one, it hurts. I don't think I'm permanently damaged, though. What are you two doing here?"

John drew himself up. "I live here, for as long as I am on this Earth. And I am your grandfather, so take a civil tone, young lady."

"You're Pops now?" I crossed my arms. "Really? Okay. What's your story?" I turned to Zane. How my eyes weren't rolling into the next town, I wasn't sure. Meema would be proud.

"We've been searching for you and your mother."

Oh, boy. Here it comes.

"Where's Meema?" Deirdre asked as she spooned eggs onto plates.

I walked around to the end of the island and sat down. "She's in Hell."

"You left her?" Daniella shouted.

"I didn't have a choice. Will you listen?" I spoke quietly. I could feel my heart speed up, and the tears were just a moment away.

Deirdre nodded and I told them everything. We ate as I talked, no one else speaking. I cried when I told them about the River of Souls. Deirdre came over and put her arms around me, and so did Daniella.

Zane looked like he'd rather be anywhere else. John wore an expression of sadness, sadder than I'd ever seen him.

"I don't know what happened to her, or what he did. I was out of it until I woke up with him laughing in my face."

"We're going to kill him," Deirdre said, wiping her eyes.

"Yes, we are," I agreed. "But first, we need to figure out a few things. Like how did I suddenly get the talent of fire?"

"Can you still do it?" Daniella asked.

"I don't know. Let me try," I got up and moved into the center of the room. Closing my eyes, I concentrated, and I felt a small sting on my hands.

"There was a small flame," Zane said. "Perhaps you need to be in a more dire situation."

"That could be. We've never been flamethrowers. I'll take it. I'd like to learn to use it in situations where I am not in imminent danger of dying."

"Add that one to the To-Do list," Daniella said with a smile. "So you don't think there's any way to get Meema back?"

I shook my head. "I don't know. I don't know anything about Hell. What about you? Aren't the dead and gone your forte?" I asked Zane.

He shrugged. "I have a good-sized library. Hell has never been one of my chief interests, because there is never any good that comes from dealing with demons. But you are welcome to look."

"It's a start. How do we kill a demon?"

"It's not going to be easy," Deirdre said. "We threw everything we had at him, and he screamed and yelled and said something I didn't understand, and then he disappeared. I thought we'd won, but then you and Meema fell to the ground and faded. So I don't know what else to do."

"Can you do the reading?" I asked Zane. "I'll agree to help you help your client." I nodded at John. "If you help us figure this out."

"Can't we just leave the demon alone?" Daniella asked.

"Well, no, we can't," I said. My skin felt itchy all over, like I was back in Hell. I didn't want to tell them, but I had to.

"Why? Because you hate that you got beat?" Daniella pushed her plate away and glared at me around Zane.

"No, because he's not going to stop."

"What do you mean?" Deirdre asked.

"He told me that since he would never get the soul of the first Desdemona, that the contract would never be fulfilled, and he was at liberty to basically harass us at will."

"That contract was very vague," Zane interjected.

"What do you mean?" I asked.

"Well, while there were specific aspects, there was a great deal of elasticity in it. That's usually a poor sign for the human signing the contract."

"I wish Granny had been around more," I sighed. "Or that Meema had shared more of this."

"Do you think she knew?" Daniella asked. "Meema seemed as surprised as we were by the contract."

"She did not know," John interrupted.

"How do you know?"

He sighed. "I will tell you, but I must make a request. It may be too much to be a grandfather, but I would appreciate it if you called me Doc."

I looked at my sisters. They nodded. Clearly, I'd missed a bunch while I'd been gone. "Okay. I guess. It may take some time," I added. "So how do you know?"

"After I died, in Glenwood Springs, I was relieved to be casting off this mortal coil. Tuberculosis was not treatable in my time. It was long, miserable death. I was pleased to be shot of my misery. Just as I was passing into the light, I felt a hook grab at me, and I was whooshed away. I came to in your grandmother's room. And there I stayed, until her death. Were Meema still here, she would tell you that she first saw me the night after the funeral. I was making noise in the room, hoping to attract some attention. I'd figured out, during the thirty-five years she kept me in there, that no one else knew about me."

"We've always known you were Meema's dad," I said.

"That was entirely due to your mother. Your grandmother told no one who the father of her child was. As a dance hall girl, no one assumed she knew."

"Are you calling Granny a whore?" I asked.

"No. But people thought what they thought. I think Desi counted on it. That way, she didn't have to tell anyone what she'd done."

"She did all this because of you."

"Darlin'," Jo— Doc said, and his gaze was kind, "she wanted to be loved, and thought I was the one to give it. I didn't have love for a single thing by that time in my life, outside my mother."

"What's happened here?" I looked around. "You're totally different than before."

"I just watched my daughter and one of my granddaughters go down fighting a demon. Trust me, it gives a man pause," Doc said.

I contemplated that. Sneaking a glance at my sisters, neither of them were wearing expressions of doubt, distrust, or aggravation. Daniella was even giving Jo—Doc a look of what could be called affection.

So, okay. I had a grandpa now. I could get behind that, as tough as it was going to be initially. But with Meema gone, the only one left who knew us, who'd been with us, was Jo— Doc. I'd have to go into my room and practice saying that a million times. We'd always been so careful to not say his name, or talk about him. But his words, and his expressions...he wasn't John anymore. He was Doc, and our family. As John, he'd been Meema's dad. But now? I couldn't explain the shift, but I felt it. His expression was sincere. All right. I had enough enemies to worry about. If he was now an ally, I'd take it.

"Fair enough. I give you my word, J—Doc, that once we sort this demon, I'll help you with whatever you want to do. I'll even work with this one." I jerked my thumb at Zane. "And that gives me pain to say. I don't have anything to do with necromancers."

"Well, it's good that you're back from Hell all changed and sweetness and light instead of your normal grumpy self," Deirdre said. "Because while you were gone, we've interrogated the daylights out of Zane. We vote he's a good addition to the neighborhood, and that you have to get over yourself."

I was so happy to be alive and with my sisters that I didn't even snap back like I had only a few days before. "Really? Tell me what changed your mind." I wasn't going to just roll over, though.

"I am a necromancer. My father was one, and that is how he raised me. But I also studied with a witch after I broke my ties with him. I prefer different magical arts. Rather than raising the dead to exploit them, I try and help them."

"Is that how you found him?" I asked Doc. I didn't mention the fact that he'd studied with a witch—one that had to agree to take him on—was compelling. He'd mentioned that before, but I hadn't been paying attention, I recalled.

"I met Doc while I was out walking."

"But I'd passed along the word I was interested in meeting," Doc added.

"To the ghost gossip hotline? Really? Those jerks. They never said a word!" No wonder all the ghosts down at Saloon 10 had avoided me that day.

"At the time, I didn't feel it was your business," Doc said. "And while I cannot leave, I have friends who pass by."

"Keep your hair on. I told you, we'll help you, if that's what you want. We need to figure out what really happened between Granny and the demon. He's not going to stop, so we need to stop him. That means I'm open to ideas," I added.

"The diaries," Doc said.

"What diaries?" Daniella asked.

"Your grandmother kept a diary every day of her life. I knew her but for a short time while alive, and even then, she wrote in it daily. Usually at night."

"Meema never said anything," Deirdre said.

"I doubt she knew. I know you all loved your grandmother, but she was a woman with many secrets," Doc said.

"Yeah, and obsessive as hell with no sense when it came to demons," I added.

"The diaries may shed some light on what really happened," Zane said. "By coming here now, so long after her death, Ashlar was able to say anything."

"Do you think the contract was fake?" I asked.

He shook his head. "No, I do not. Demons take their bargains seriously. But as I said, that contract was written by Ashlar, and it was written in his favor. I am sorry to tell you, but your grandmother never had a chance."

"Even shady jerks like Ashlar?" Deirdre asked.

"Well, she beat him. She got away," I said. "Even if that means we're doomed."

"I think there may be some hope. Not a lot. But Doc may be right," Zane said. "The diaries may hold a key that sends us to the information we need. I'll go home and start reading and see what I can find. They are magical, and descended from God, so demons are hard to kill. But everything has to die. I'll come by later and let you know what I find."

We all said goodbye and watched him go. As the door closed behind him, Daniella said, "I'm glad you're not being an ass, Desi, because he's a good guy. He's been here every day offering to help since you and Meema disappeared."

"We need to find the diaries," I said to Doc. "We need to get ready. Ashlar is going to figure out that I'm gone sooner than I'd like, if he doesn't know already. He'll be back."

"We need to lay Meema to rest," Deirdre said. "That comes first."

"Are you crazy? That needs to happen, but we need to be ready. I don't think you understand. This guy was gleeful at having hundreds of years to torture me. And he is gunning for all of us! He's not going to see that I've gotten away and think oh, well, too bad for me!" I could feel the panic rising. How could they not see what was coming?

"We have to live in this town," Daniella said. "I know you're scared, but have you forgotten that? Whatever we do, we still have to live here if we want the kind of life we've built for ourselves. So we need to think of that in addition to getting ready for the demon."

"We could leave," I said.

"Now I know you're not thinking straight," Deirdre said. "Yeah, we could leave. But we lose everything that we need to fight against this guy. We're sitting ducks if we leave. We have to stay here. It's where we can have the ability to fight back. And why should we leave because he's all bent out of shape?"

The world was upside down. I was normally the one with the reasonable lines. But right now, all I could think was that I didn't want to go back to Hell. I really, really wanted to stay here. "You're right. If we leave, we have nothing that will fight him."

"Why don't you go sleep some more, and Dani and I will come up with something. I think Meema might have blown herself up in an accident in the shop. She was so crazy with her herbal experiments," Deirdre added with a smile. "And this won't take long, Desi. We are also totally capable of multi-tasking."

It was funny because it was true. Meema did a lot of spell creation and casting in the back room of the store. She'd blown her eyebrows off more than once.

"That would be a good cover," I said. I could feel myself moving away from the blind panic.

"You'll need a body," Doc said quietly.

"We can manage that as well," Daniella said. "Go sleep, Desi. You need it. We don't know what Hell did to you. It might not show up right away."

I was about to protest when I yawned so hard my jaw cracked. I thought about my reaction just a couple of minutes ago. Hell had done something to me. I couldn't keep going off like this, or I'd hurt us more than anything else. "Okay. I'm not going to fight."

"Thank the goddess for small miracles," Deirdre said. "First time for everything. I think sending you to Hell might have been the thing we all needed."

"Shut up," I said, throwing my napkin at her. "Just for that, I'm not touching the dishes." I got up and started back to my room.

"You're just adding on more later," Deirdre and Daniella said in unison, in a perfect imitation of Meema's voice.

It was exactly what I needed. My worry wasn't gone, but we had a plan. That was a good place to start.

CHAPTER SEVEN

When I woke up, the clock told me I'd slept for about five hours. It was still daylight outside, and the house seemed to be intact, which meant Ashlar hadn't shown up yet. I knew he was coming back. It was only a matter of time.

Downstairs, it was quiet, and no one was around. No one had left a note, which I found annoying.

"They're all down at the shop, or the funeral parlor, or some such." Doc drifted into the kitchen.

"Thanks," I said. "I'm trying to remember to call you Doc," I added. "John is habit."

"Well, I haven't been much of a family member. I've had my own concerns that have made me ... surly a great deal."

"That's one way of putting it," I agreed.

"It's not as though you girls ever treated me as family," he shot back.

I forgot, sometimes, how quick he was. That had been his reputation when he was alive, and he hadn't lost that when he died.

He continued, "I think you're ashamed of me. You don't use

my name, even though I'm the only male with any blood relation in this family."

He was right. Meema had married a man that she told us was not our father, and he hadn't been a big part of our lives. She'd never told us exactly who our father was, and after a while, we stopped asking. We had her and Granny and it didn't seem to matter.

"I don't think you understand," I said as I poured cereal and then milk into my bowl.

"Enlighten me." He crossed his arms and there wasn't an ounce of give in his manner.

"There's a thing with you. With your memory. With the idea of who you are. Or were," I added. "It's been like that for ages. After you died, the papers, and then the media, got on the Doc Holliday bandwagon. You're a folk hero. As far as the rest of the world knows, you don't have any children. There are theories, but none of them ever landed anywhere near here, and we like it that way."

"You're ashamed of me," he said flatly as though I hadn't said one single word.

"No, I am not. I don't want all the notoriety that would come with telling anyone. In addition to all the people who would think we were lying."

"So you are saying you do not want publicity?"

"Doc, you've been here, all this time, with us. When have we ever sought out publicity? Granny, and then Meema, had enough to keep us on the rails, and make it look like we're a couple of generations more than we really are, and stop the old biddies who thought one of us was looking at her tired old husband." This whole other-women's-husbands thing was kind of a theme here. It's tough, when you're living down dance hall girl ancestors in a small town. Even though Granny, for all her batshit crazy, was worth ten of most of the people here.

He laughed, and it transformed his face.

I realized that I hadn't seen a lot of Doc in happy situations. "Have you been so unhappy here?"

"I have, indeed. But after I watched you and Little Desi—"

"Little Desi?" I interrupted.

"That is how I referred to your mother, even though Desdemona never allowed me to see her while she herself was alive."

"Have you seen Granny since she died?" I asked, getting us further off topic.

"No. She knew of my anger. She knew I wanted to be free, and she refused. She always said to me that she was promised love, and since I was there, that's where I was going to be. I never understood that, although I do now."

"She didn't tell you about Ashlar?"

"Would you have shared such information?"

"Good point. Back to you. I'm sorry you've been miserable."

"And I am sorry that I have added to the misery around this house. That creature, that demon"—Doc shook his head—"explains so much that I never understood. Your mother knew, I believe, that your grandmother had done something less than decent. I do not believe she knew the extent of matters."

"I'll agree with that. I think Meema was as shocked as we were. Granny is the key here. We need to find her diaries."

"We will need to search both her room and your mother's room."

I sagged against the counter. That felt really disrespectful. Meema was barely gone. My eyes welled up—I was crying more in this week than I had in fifty years—and I rubbed at them.

"I know this all seems too soon, darlin', but I happen to agree with your assessment of the demon. He is not going to be pleased to find you gone. He will return here."

The fear that I'd been able to push away returned and hit me like a sledgehammer. "I can't go back there, Doc. I won't. I'll kill myself before I let him win, much less drag me back."

"I understand. Let us hope it doesn't get to that point. I will do all I can to help you. It may not be much, mind you," he added.

"Why the sudden change?"

He looked thoughtful, knowing exactly what I was referring to. "When I saw the demon attack the three of you, I realized that while your grandmother and I may have become enemies, I enjoyed her greatly while I lived here. She was a lively woman, full of spirit. And she had my daughter. She didn't tell me, which was probably wise of her. It made me sad to think that she did all this because she wanted my love so badly. That want became twisted, and warped. I asked myself then, what had I ever done to better things? What had I ever done to make things right? With her, with your mother, with you girls? I'd done nothing. And I realized how much I loved your mother, my daughter. How much I loved you all. How proud I was of you. Then I realized what a fool I'd been, carrying a grudge all these years. I decided that I was changing my ways. Granted, it's been all of five days," he smiled, "But I'm a changed man."

"Do you still want to go?"

"I cannot answer that at this time. I do not know. I know that I cannot leave you all to face this on your own. I have a hand in these dealings, and regardless of what may have been said, I did not cheat, and I played my cards to the end."

"Great. You think this is the end?"

"I do not. I have seen all of you do a great deal over the years. You're strong and smart. I think you have the best shot of defeating this demon."

"Do you trust Zane?"

He wasn't expecting that. "I beg your pardon?"

"Do you trust Zane? You know, the necromancer you hired?"

"I do indeed. I will confess, I hired him in a moment of desperation, where I would have hired Sallie the dog if the opportunity presented itself. But his behavior since you and Little Desi disappeared has been that of a gentleman."

"What did you and Meema argue about?"

"I asked her to help me go. She told me she didn't know how. I told her that her damned mother had done this, so she could right things. She disagreed. I told her I'd take matters into my own hands, then, and at that point, the conversation ended."

I'd been right. They'd argued over this. Which was why Meema had told me not to just pop off and beat the necromancer down. I didn't think the argument had been that simple, but he could keep his secrets in this. I didn't think he was hiding anything we had to know. At least, I hoped not.

"We need to find those diaries. You said she wrote in them every day?"

"She did indeed. She wrote a great deal at night, and sometimes she would cry. Again, I wonder what part I played in that, and if I shall regret helping you to find them." He smiled at me, but it was a sad smile. "It is never pleasant to revisit the scenes of one's past, particularly if that past puts them in an unflattering light."

"You were a shit to her, weren't you? When you lived here, in Deadwood?"

Doc shrugged. "From my vantage point now, yes. At the time, I was on borrowed time. I determined that I should live as I pleased. I made no promises to any women. How could I? I was a walking death sentence."

"Fair enough. You know, we have never talked like this, ever, in all the time I've been alive."

"It's been a house of secrets."

"Yeah, well, that ends. Secrets are what got us into this mess. Come on, let's go find these damn diaries and see what further mess Granny left us." My tone was mild. But I hoped he'd gotten the warning. I was done with secrets popping up on the lawn and dragging me off to Hell.

Something Doc had said struck me. Granny had been full of life and spirit when he met her, and he'd had fun with her. She'd obviously changed. I'd seen women go crazy for love, and had a few of them in our shop, demanding a love potion. It was never pretty. It made me sad to think Granny might have gone that way. But considering the deal she'd made with Ashlar, it looked like that was exactly what happened. I didn't have a good memory of it. We'd been barely ten when she died.

We went up to Granny's room, which was where Meema had moved into after we got older. The house had been moved since Granny died, so where the diaries might have ended up was anyone's guess. But we'd emptied the house, and as far as I knew, Meema hadn't said she'd found them.

Would she tell us if she had? This family mystery took on more layers and crap every moment. I wish I knew what Meema had known.

If she had, she would have hidden them in her room, away from us. It didn't make sense though. Doc was right. Meema had been shocked at the agreement Ashlar showed us.

Two hours later, with no sign of my sisters, I collapsed on the floor of Meema's room. "I don't know where she could have hidden this, Doc. We've been over the entire room."

Doc looked thoughtful. He'd even passed through the floors to see if he could see anything, and come up empty.

"Where did she put the diary after she finished writing in it? You said she wrote at night, right?"

"It was by her bedside. I am afraid I didn't pay much attention to what I thought was the writing of women."

"Sometimes you're just a peach," I said.

"I prefer a daisy. And yes, I am."

I threw one of Meema's slippers that I'd pushed aside to crawl under the bed at him. It went right through him.

"That's extremely rude."

"I'm feeling extremely rude. Where the hell are these—" I stopped. Getting up, I went out into the hall. Our house was built in 1884. There was a large cupboard in the hallway where linens were stored. It was a massive wooden built-in with two large, ornate doors. The cupboard on the right extended to the outer wall of the house, and there was a compartment cut into it. We never knew who had done it but it was a great place to hide things.

I tore into the cupboard, pulling out blankets, and curtains, and who knew what else. There, at the bottom and back, was the small trap door I remembered. We'd tried to put Deirdre in there once, and Meema had almost whipped us. Almost. Whippings never were much of a deterrent to us. Not even Deana, who was the most mild-mannered.

I lifted the trap. A black metal box sat in the bottom. I took it out, and leaned down into the hole. Using my phone, I shone a flashlight to see if there was anything else. There was. Four more black metal boxes. One by one, I pulled them out. They were not too heavy, but whatever was in them was solid, and didn't rattle.

"Goddess, please let these be the diaries." If these boxes didn't have them tucked away I'd have to go through the entire house. I didn't even want to contemplate it.

Once I was sure the small cubby was empty, I backed out of the cupboard, and put the linens back. Doc observed all this.

"Aren't you dying to see what is in there?" He looked at me incredulously.

"I'm going to look, but if it's them, I'm not going to read them yet." They were all locked, and I used an unlatching spell to open all five. Who knew where the keys were?

As I opened the first, my heart raced. There were notebooks. Seven or eight of them, maybe? I opened the top of it and saw the date.

"Well?" Doc asked.

"It's them. We should get Daniella and Deirdre back here." I called Deirdre's cell.

"Hey, you're up. How are you feeling?" She sounded pleased.

"I found the diaries," I said.

"What? Already? Oh holy— hang on." She must have covered the mic, because I could hear her talking to someone else, but I couldn't understand what she said. "Okay, we're done here. We're heading back now." She hung up.

"They're on the way."

"Good. I confess that I am mightily interested in what is in those diaries."

I picked up the boxes, stacking them carefully one on top of the other, and then walked slowly down the stairs to the dining room table. "We're going to need to read fast. The clock is ticking. I can't believe Ashlar hasn't come back yet."

"Your sisters have a point. You have to still carry on your life here." Doc sounded almost as though he were issuing a warning.

"If we don't figure out a way to end this, I—we—won't have a life here! Yeah, he's after me, but he made it clear all the Nightingales were fair game. Oh, shit," I said as another thought struck me. Deana's girls. They didn't know.

"What?"

"I need to talk to Deirdre and Dani. I can't make this call alone."

"For what?"

I waved off his question. I wasn't ready to face this one yet. Oh, goddess. We had to let them know that Meema was gone. While Deana had left us, and she was long gone, her daughter and granddaughters were still here. I knew that Meema spoke with them regularly. Had spoken. The tears threatened again.

With an optimism that was perhaps misplaced, I set a box

at each place at the table and wiped at my face. “We need to get Zane over here. That way, each of us can go through the diaries in one box. And there’s only one left over.”

Daniella came in the front door, followed by Deirdre.

“Can one of you call Zane? We’re going to need his help.”

“He may have his own stuff to tend to, Desi.”

“Not unless he wants a demon galloping all over the place.”

One of them muttered something in response, but I couldn’t make it out, and I didn’t take the bait. Daniella called Zane, and she said loudly, “What? Stop, Zane, you need to say that again, because I don’t think I heard you right.”

We all looked over at her. She pointed at the phone, trying to tell me something, but I wasn’t getting it. She nodded, then said, “Well, bring him over, I guess. Yeah, she mentioned it, but…holy Joseph. Okay. *OKAY*. See you soon.”

“What?” I asked.

“What was the name of the demon who helped you?”

“Beeval,” I said.

Evil, hearing what he thought was his name, clucked, and came in to stroll through and check out the activity. His feathers brushed against my leg. “Not you,” I said. “It’s not all about you, Evil. No, the demon’s name is Beeval. He said he would follow me out, but he disappeared. I wasn’t sure if he was trying to set me up, but I felt bad. He looked like misery walking.”

“Yeah, well, it’s time to find out,” Daniella gave me a half-grin. “Because he showed up on Zane’s doorstep.”

“What?” I couldn’t believe it. “How did he get away?”

Daniella shrugged. “I don’t know. He’s coming over with Zane, so you can ask him. I know he helped you, but we need to set up a protection spell. And Evil, shoo!” She ran at the chicken, sending him into the back of the house. “Demons like chicken.”

“Evil would win,” I said, laughing.

"Probably, but I'd rather not test that theory." Daniella shut the door behind Evil, and we all waited for Zane. With the demon.

Who I hoped was a friend. I'd hate to hurt him. The look in his eyes wouldn't leave me. Had he come bearing some horrible surprise gift to further hurt me?

No. I couldn't—wouldn't—believe it. I wasn't that bad a judge of character.

A knock on the door, and then Zane came in. Behind him was the small demon. In the light, he was a blackish brown. Same eyes, same long nose. He seemed even more frightened than before.

I walked around Zane to kneel down in front of Beeval. "How did you get here?"

"Tunnel. I wait, and then I come."

"Why didn't you come with me?"

"Must watch Ashlar."

"Does he know I am gone?"

"He busy. Big boss give him lots to do. You were fun, not work."

That was interesting. It also made me wonder if Ashlar was up to something his boss or overlord wouldn't approve of. A thought to file away. "So he doesn't know yet?"

"Still my turn to watch. I lose fight, so I watch."

That had been what the scuffling was all about. Beeval got the short straw, basically, and none of them had come back. Well, fear was not a great motivator for good job performance. I smiled at him. "You got away."

"I did." He smiled.

Which was a little disconcerting, given his teeth. I didn't care. I put my arms around him. He smelled like Hell, and brimstone, and sautéed onion. "You are welcome here," I said. "For as long as you want."

There was a cough from one of my sisters, but I ignored it. This one wasn't up for a vote.

"You in danger." His large eyes searched my face.

"I know."

"I help."

"You already have. What do you need to be here?"

"Food. Hiding place. Dark."

The light must be killing him. "I have the perfect place for you," I said. "What do you want to do now?"

"Sleep?" he asked slowly.

I realized that he must not get asked a lot.

"Doc, would you take him to the hidey hole we just found?"

Doc smiled. "Good idea. But I can't move the linens and things."

"Oh, hell." I felt weird saying that now. "Right. Never mind. I'll do it. Tell them about the diaries. Beeval, you come with me."

He reached out one of his long arms to me, and I took his claw. Even though he was a creature of Hell, I knew he was meant to be here. I knew this was the right decision. I might need some time to convince Deirdre and Daniella of that, however.

We walked up the stairs together, hand in claw. I pointed at the large cupboard. "This is where you can stay. It's dark, it's quiet, and no one will bother you here. When you're ready, you come out," I said, taking the blankets and towels and various other linens out. I used my phone flashlight to show him the hidey hole.

He peered in and smiled at me again. For a demon to look so sweet, the Earth must have fallen off its axis, or something. Or I bumped my head really hard. But he did look sweet.

"I have?" He gestured at a pile of blankets.

"Uh, sure?"

He leaped down from the cupboard and grabbed them, dragging them back to the hidey hole.

"You come out whenever you're ready, okay?"

"Yes. Thank you, Desimo."

"No, Beeval. Thank you. You saved my life."

He made a humming noise that I guess meant it was all good, patted my leg, and disappeared into the hidey hole, pulling the cover over top of him. I looked at the pile of linens still on the floor. I couldn't leave them here, because that would drive me crazy. I shoved them over to the left side and closed the door, leaving it open a crack so Beeval could see it when he woke up.

Then I went back downstairs to find my past.

CHAPTER EIGHT

Everyone had taken a seat around the table, except Doc, who hovered. I sat down across from Deirdre. "Did Doc tell you?"

"What he could."

"Before we get into this, how did things end between you and..." Zane stopped.

"Granny," I said.

"Yes. You and Granny."

We all looked at Doc. He sighed. "Very well. If you must know. I fear for the version we're about to read."

"Get on with it," Daniella said.

"I came up here in 1876. My friend, Tom Miller, he was of the notion to open a Bella Union Saloon, since it had done so well in Cheyenne. I came with him, having secured a deal for the faro tables. The Bella did well, as it was more respectable than the Gem. That was a proper blood bath," he added. "I met your grandmother at the Bella. I never thought Desdemona Nightingale was her name, but she never gave me another. I called her Desi. We enjoyed our time together. She was a quick study at the cards."

"She won this house in a game of cards," I said.

"I know. It makes me proud. I left something good for her."

"Two things," Deirdre said.

Doc stopped and looked at her. He caught on, and his mouth opened, and closed. "That is most kind of you to say. As I was saying, we got on well. She was light, and lively, and happy. Until I told her that I was of a mind to head south once more. I did not know then, but at that point, our association had... borne fruit." He pursed his lips.

I started to laugh. "I'm sorry, but that is such a funny way to say it."

Daniella covered her mouth to hide the smile.

"I didn't realize you were missish," Deirdre said to Doc.

"I am not. But I am respectful of mothers."

"Did she tell you?" I asked.

"No, she did not. I told you that. I think it was a wise choice on her part. She begged me to stay, told me she could help me with the consumption. I told her I'd seen every quack east and west of the Mississippi, and that I would pass. She was angry, but there was more. It was almost a panic."

"She knew she was pregnant, and she was scared," I said. I could see it, and I couldn't. My memories of Granny were of a strong, no-nonsense woman. She'd been kind of scary. Meema smiled and laughed a lot more than Granny ever did.

"No doubt. The hell of it is, if she'd made the deal with that devil she probably could have helped me. She must have had the magic then. I brushed it off, and shortly after that, I left. The last time I saw her, she was crying without making a sound. She didn't say anything, just watched me go." Doc turned his head away.

I thought he might be ashamed. But I wasn't going to assume, and I sure as shit wasn't going to say anything. Our talk this afternoon left me feeling unsettled, and good, all at the same time.

"Did you see her again?" Zane asked.

"No. I went south, and I took up with Kate then. There was no more time for any other woman. Kate would have run them off."

We were all silent. I felt sorry for Granny. Alone, pregnant, and she'd lost the man she loved. Doc was right—she must have made the deal by then, since she thought she could save Doc. And she was a dance hall girl. We'd lived with that growing up, back when we were still ourselves. No one let us forget our granny was a saloon girl, said with all the attitude you can imagine. And Granny was alone.

"When I died, your mother was nearly ten years old. Desi had been raising her on her own all that time. It would not have been easy. An unmarried woman would not have found much kindness. Well, when I died, I saw the light that I'd always heard about. I was astounded as I never assumed I'd see such a sight. And then I saw Desi. I said something, I don't remember what—"

"'This is funny.' That's what you said," Deirdre interrupted.

"I guess. I remember thinking this wasn't what I expected, but I do not recall. I didn't expect to see her. Something that felt like a hook around my middle pulled me, pulled me away from the light. When I came to, I was in your Granny's room, and she was looking at me, rocking in her rocking chair."

"What happened?" Daniella asked.

"She told me that I would be with her always because that was the bargain she made. I said that I had made no such bargain, and that it was my time to go. Her face closed up. I know you all know the look. It was as though a door slammed in front of me. I shouted that I'd damn well leave if I damn well wanted to. She said that I was confined to this room until I could behave better. That she wouldn't risk all that she'd built because I was being difficult. And she walked out. I was in her room for thirty-five years. She did agree, about ten years in when we were driving each other mad, that I could walk around the house. But no one else could see me. I discovered that while she was not in the house, I could not leave the room."

"She was powerful," Zane said. "That is very strong magic."

"More than we realized," I added.

"When your Granny died, I was still trapped in the room. She wasn't in the home. It was due to me making noise and your mother coming in to gain my freedom. But then I discovered that not only could I not leave this Earthly plane, I couldn't even leave the backyard. Your mother was ... very low-key in her reception of me. I imagine that she had Granny's impressions. I never brought up leaving again. I figured that I would need to find a way to escape."

"And you never did?" Deirdre asked.

"Nothing that would break Desi's spell," Doc muttered.

"Okay then. With that, we need to get into the diaries. You ready for this?" I asked my sisters.

"No," Deirdre said.

"Yes," Daniella replied at the same time. "I'm tired of all the secrets. If we'd known all this, we might have found a way to handle this a long time ago."

"I totally agree. Let's see what the real deal was with Granny."

For the next two hours we read.

I learned that Granny had been madly in love with Doc. The diaries began when she moved to Deadwood. She'd never told us much about her family, but it was in here. She'd been orphaned by cholera, and she wasn't all that upset about her. Her father had run off, and her mother seemed angry a great deal. Granny was glad to be able to leave their life behind.

There was an entry the night she met Doc.

"I have secured a good position as a dancer at the new Bella Union Saloon. Mr. Miller is strict about the customers roughing up

the girls, so there is a bit more safety than a place like the Gem. I'm happy with my place here. And I have met the most wonderful man. His name is John Holliday, from Georgia. When he speaks, I can hear the birds, feel the sunshine, and smell the peaches. He is delightful and ever the gentleman. The papers have called him the notorious Doc Holliday, but he is so gentle and polite with me. I think I am falling in love. Who would have thought this would happen to me, little Desdemona Nightingale?"

I wouldn't show this to Doc. It would hurt him, and that wouldn't do a damn bit of good now. All the coldness I'd felt for him was easing. Whatever he'd done to Granny, he had paid for it. So had she. They'd paid for it ten times over, the both of them.

Daniella gave a shout. "I found something!"

"Read it," I said.

"I have come upon a solution. Mrs. Cannady and her daughter Amelia are both consumptive. Mrs. Cannady has four younger children. Neither of them have a year left. Six months at best. I am going to offer to help them go peacefully, and promise to take care of the children. I will, of course. Mrs. C is a good mother, and as a mother myself, I completely understand."

Daniella said, "About two months later, there's this: *It is done. I have sent the Cannadys on their way. Ashlar came for them, and within a moment, he'd whisked their souls from their bodies. I took the entire family in, to treat the two sick women, so them passing on my front porch will not be seen as out of the ordinary. I have already arranged for the children to be cared for. I offered to raise them myself, but Mrs. C said that would look odd. So she made arrangements with an older childless couple, and I secured a lawyer and gave them all a dowry. I also promised I'd make sure they kept honest, and I will. Those children will not suffer."*

"So she did it," I said. "She really did send two other women in her place to die."

"They were going to die anyway," Doc said. "That was a guarantee."

"You haven't been to Hell," I shot back. "That was not a picnic, and it sure wasn't a reward."

Doc and I glared at one another.

"We need to find something about her bargain with the demon," Zane said.

With that reminder, we got back to reading. An hour later, we stopped to eat some dinner. Then it was right back to reading.

Finally, I found it. What we were looking for.

"I have been searching for ways to kill Ashlar. He will eventually figure things out, and while he is not the smartest demon—I've dealt with far superior demons since—he will learn the truth. I hope the C's have been able to keep it from him as long as possible. My spy tells me they are both still there. He has, as a payment of a favor to me, been easing their suffering for several years, but who knows how time goes in H? So I must prepare to face him when—not if—he comes back." I stopped, and looked around.

"Well?" Doc said. "What does she suggest?"

"*To kill a demon, the talents of those in the mortal world will not work. I have spoken with my acquaintance in the realms of Hell and I know this to be true. He might not be completely honest—"*

"She was still messing about with demons? I am so not feeling all that sorry for her!" Deirdre exclaimed, tossing down the diary she was reading. "Didn't she learn anything? I mean she had to send two innocent women to their deaths because of her interaction with Ashlar!"

"Let me finish," I said. She had a spy." That was interesting to me, and I read ahead for a moment. "*He might not be completely honest, but he loathes Ashlar, and would be pleased to see him gone. He has told me, and I have verified this with more than one witch, as well as several necromancers, that I must find an angelic sword. I was not aware there were such things, and I have been told they are rare, and well-hidden. So I must find one. Outside of that, there is only one other way. I shall have to allow him to take my soul. While I could agree to that, I cannot do that to my darling Desdemona. I am so sorry, my sweet girl, that I ever agreed to such a thing for you. It was not right of me to gamble with your life."* I stopped again. "She wasn't completely batshit crazy."

"Yeah, well, hindsight is really a lovely thing. The deed was done by then." Deirdre looked away in disgust.

"There is no choice. I must find the sword. As I stared out the window today, I see that Little Desi has returned from her walk with Jack Fitzgerald. He is a sweet boy, for all that he thinks he will make his fortune in mining. I expect that they will be engaged soon."

"That's not a name we've heard before," Daniella said. "I wonder if that's the mystery baby daddy."

"You are awfully cavalier about your sire," Doc said. He sounded very stiff.

"We didn't know our dad. It was always Meema and Granny. Meema was married for a while, to Nicholas Burns, but he wasn't around long. We always had them, and then it was Meema. And you," Deirdre added.

Doc didn't say anything. It's hard at times to decipher the nuances of a ghost's expression. I decided to table this particular conversational avenue and get back to the matter at hand. "We need to find an angel sword. That's it, then? Nothing else? Nothing else is going to kill the demons?"

"We need to figure out who Granny's source was," Daniella said. "Maybe he'd like another shot at offing Ashlar."

"I have heard of angel's swords, but I've never seen one," said Zane.

I was starting to like him. He was quiet, thoughtful, he wasn't overly pushy, and he seemed to say things that were logical and made sense. No crazy or histrionics. The Nightingales needed no help in that department. "I am going to assume they're not just lying around waiting for someone to need one, are they? They're probably locked up tight somewhere with a thousand gross things guarding them."

"That sounds about right." Zane smiled.

"Well, we are going to need to beat the odds, beat the bushes, and shake one free," I said. "Because I am not going back to Hell. I'm not letting him take either of you," I met the eyes of both my sisters. "And speaking of which, we need to call Deana."

"Which one?" Deirdre asked.

"The oldest. Our niece."

"Who is Deana?" Zane asked.

"Our other sister. Somehow, Meema managed to have four live babies. I'm wondering if Granny didn't have something to do with that, too, since her fingers seemed to be in every pie around here. But Deana got totally pissed about all the wacky magic, and the rules—"

"What are the rules?" he interrupted.

"Use your magic for good. Do no harm to the innocent. Do not work with those who are evil. Protect Deadwood, no exceptions." Deirdre, Daniella, and I chorused together.

Zane smiled. As I watched him, I realized I hadn't really seen his smile before. Well, since we'd met, there hadn't been a lot to smile about. He'd smiled a little, a few times. But as he smiled now, I felt myself drawn to his attractiveness. As though he knew what I was thinking his eyes flickered toward me. The intensity of his gaze rippled through me, and I had to look away.

This was neither the time nor the place. And certainly not with a necromancer, no matter how good looking. "So. Angel sword. Where exactly do we find one?"

No one answered me.

"Come on. That's what we have to do. We can't let this douchebag run all over us, and harass us until we beg him to drag us off to his stinky lair. That's just not going to work for me. We have to find this spy friend of Granny's." I looked around the table.

"I wonder if the demon has seen an angel sword," Zane mused. He sounded like he was thinking out loud more than anything else.

"You can ask him when he wakes up, as long as you ask nicely."

Deirdre pushed the diary she'd been reading away from her, and her chair away from the table. "I'm done with this. We know the deal. Granny was lovesick and stupid. Sorry, Doc, but she was. I don't care how nicely you rubbed her bunions, or whatever—and the demon had all kinds of add on shit that he oopsed on telling Granny. So he cheated her. Then she cheated him. Since he's the last one standing, he's got his hand out, and going to be a pain in our ass. What else do we need to know right now?"

Everyone stared. Then I started to laugh. "You're right, Deeds. One hundred percent right. We know what happened. We know he's a stinky douche—"

"You're really hung up on this stinky thing," Zane said, the corners of his mouth quirking up.

"If you'd smelled him in Hell, you'd understand that I am not nearly hung up enough. Did you get a whiff of Beeval? He's adorable, but he needs a bath in the worst way."

"Yeah, can we talk about the demon?" Daniella put down her diary. "I'm not trying to be a jerk, because he did save your life, but are you really serious about letting him stay here?"

"I am. He did save me. And he was miserable. He doesn't belong there."

"Demons do, in fact, come from Hell, correct?" Doc asked.

"Yes," Deirdre said. "That's their place in the world."

"Well, that's not Beeval's place! He's staying." I glared at my sisters.

Then Daniella said, "He better not go near Evil. That's all

I'm saying. And you better talk to him. Because I'm not keeping Evil locked in the back of the house. And you're cleaning up the extra poop," she added.

"That's fine. I know it's weird, and goes against everything that we know, but all this"—I indicated the diaries—"shows us that we're not in the full know. So maybe we need to be a little more flexible?"

Deirdre sighed. "Fine. Have your big-nosed little demon."

"His nose is cute."

"Whatever. He's your deal."

I smiled. For the first time in forever, we weren't fighting. No dishes were thrown. I'd give almost anything to have Meema throw a dish at me again, but since that wasn't in the cards, I'd take the peace my sisters and I had tacitly agreed to. "I hate to be the specter at the feast, here, but we need to call the Deanas."

"Crap. I forgot about them." Daniella had a frown on her face. "What are we going to tell them?"

"The truth. Don't you think it's about time?" I asked.

"Yes, but they aren't into our way of life, remember? And do we really want to worry them?"

"They're Nightingales, right?"

"Of course," Deirdre said.

"Then they are in danger, too. And they have a right to know. You know, we could invite them here."

"To get them killed?"

"To let them be a part of it. To be here for the funeral, too."

"Who would want to be a part if this if they could avoid it?" Doc asked.

"You do not understand tact in the moment, do you?" I replied.

"I am asking a reasonable question. You may give me my head back now."

"Then you have to make the call," Daniella said. "I'm never

sure what to say. I know why Deana said she left, and I feel like she had to tell her daughter and granddaughters."

"Which is fine. Meema was never mad at her."

Both of my sisters sighed. "You're right," Deirdre said. "And she could have been the angriest. All right. Go call her. We'll listen and criticize you when you're done."

I laughed again. "There's my sister I know and annoy. I'm ready for a break from these anyway." Getting up, I pulled out my cell phone and went out back to call my niece.

She answered on the second ring. "Aunt Desi? How are you?"

"I'm all right, Deana, but I'm not calling with the best of news."

Her voice changed. "Do you ever?"

Oh, Deana had indeed been telling stories. Those three words said it all.

"Meema has passed away."

There was silence, and then she caught her breath. She didn't say anything and it dawned on me that she was crying.

"I'm sorry," I said.

"When is the funeral?"

"Tomorrow. It's sudden, but we—"

"We'll be there," she said, and she hung up.

I walked back into the kitchen.

"That was quick. Well?" Daniella said.

"Not quite cold as ice, but definitely icy. They'll be here for the funeral tomorrow."

"Shit. You sure about this? I'm really nervous," Daniella stated. "They're not prepared for what could be coming."

"We'll spell the entire town," I exclaimed. "If all four of us, yes, you, too, Zane, cast a protection spell, along with a repelling and a do no harm mixed in there, it will make it really difficult for him to drop by." There was no need to specify which 'him' I referred to.

"That kind of spell is going to take some work," Zane said.

"And a lot of energy," Deirdre said. "We might need to make some boosters."

"What are boosters?" Asked Zane.

"Nightingale secrets," I said before either of my sisters just handed him our spells. Just because he was nice, and smart, and attractive, and laughed appealingly didn't mean he got our family secrets.

He nodded. He didn't look offended, but what did I know? The last time I'd seriously looked at a man, I'd been all of twenty-nine. Really twenty-nine, not the many-generations-later twenty-nine I'd been through a couple of times.

Meema had sat us all down, before our twenty-first birthday and explained that we'd never die, as long as we lived here. We didn't know it then, but that was when Deana had decided to leave. She knew even then she didn't want immortality. She wanted more than Deadwood. I respected it, but I didn't understand it.

Anyway, Meema also told us we needed to be careful with men. That we wouldn't age, not like humans, and not like our men. That eventually our men, even if they were not the most observant, would notice that we weren't aging. So we needed to consider how we wanted to manage our romantic lives.

It was a pretty shitty conversation when all you think about is men.

A month later, Deana left, and wrote us from Los Angeles. She said she loved us all, but she wanted more.

I was angry at her for leaving. At the time, it had felt like she was turning her back on her responsibility to Deadwood. I didn't tell her that, though. But even before she left, she told me that she hadn't felt obligated to take on something just because Granny and Meema did it.

Which meant who knew what she'd told her daughters and granddaughters? Then I shrugged my shoulders. The Deanas would need to get their shit together, or sit down and shut up. It was that simple. If they'd come here to judge, that would be their crap to manage.

I—we—had more than enough to manage without all sorts of family drama. Which included a funeral none of us had ever expected tomorrow.

CHAPTER NINE

After the phone call to the Deanas, we'd all stepped away from the diaries. Deirdre and Daniella, rising almost as one, got up.

"I'm going to shower, pick out something to wear, and going to bed," Daniella said.

"Make that two," Deirdre added.

"That's my cue to leave," Zane said.

"You're welcome back tomorrow," I said before I was aware of it. My face warmed, and I could see Deirdre and Daniella watching me. I didn't like that. The questions would be coming.

"Are you sure? I don't want to intrude," he said.

"I'm sure."

"Gee, we're not out for blood with the necromancer neighbor now?" Deirdre asked, teasing me.

"No. I have decided you don't need to die immediately." I smiled at Zane.

His expression lightened. "Well, that's a relief. I have a roast in the oven."

A moment of silence greeted his statement, and then everyone, even Doc, started to laugh.

“So I’ll go and tend to it,” Zane finished.

“You might need to come cook for us,” Daniella said. “Meema was the cook. None of us are all that good.”

“How old are you three?” Zane asked. “And you don’t cook?”

“Meema didn’t want us in her kitchen.” I shrugged. “You’re right, though—we’re going to need to learn to feed ourselves.”

“And the demon,” Deirdre muttered. “Don’t forget him.”

“Yeah, I don’t know what he eats. Shit. That’s another thing to figure out. Anyway, come back tomorrow around eight. We have to leave after then. You’re welcome to sit with us.”

“I’m not family.” Zane sounded stiff.

“You tried to save her,” I countered. “You can sit with family.”

He nodded, and left, shutting the door quietly behind him. There was silence after he left, and then Daniella took two steps to the window, peering out.

“Okay, he’s gone. It’s time to talk about this, Desi.”

“Talk about what?” I crossed my arms.

“You like him,” Deirdre said, her lips turned up in a smile. “Don’t try to beat around the bush. You like him.”

“What if I do?” I was too tired to argue.

“I think it would be great. Just think, you could date without having to worry about exposing yourself. Well, not in the bad ways, anyway.” Daniella grinned.

“You do seem fond of him for all your words,” Doc observed.

“He’s not your standard necromancer. I’m glad I didn’t kill him. I wouldn’t have Beeval,” I added.

“I’m not sure that’s a plus,” Deirdre said.

“He doesn’t seem all that bad,” Doc said.

“Yeah, until he takes a bite out of Evil, and I blast him,” Daniella said.

“I’ll keep them away from each other,” I said. One more thing to worry over.

Doc drifted closer. "You look tired. You all do. Why don't you go to bed, and I'll wake you if anything needs to be handled. Demon, chicken, other demon—don't worry, girls. I'll wake you."

As one, we nodded, and my sisters scattered to go to their rooms. Doc was right. I was tired. And I was sure Deirdre and Daniella were too. They didn't have the distraction of the field trip to Hell, but this had been a rough week.

I lingered in the kitchen. "Thank you," I said to Doc. "We need this."

"I know, darlin'. I know. Get some sleep. But I'm waking you up if the little demon gets up."

"You know, eventually everyone will appreciate that I let him stay." I crossed my arms.

Doc chuckled. "Perhaps. Not at the moment."

"Yeah, yeah." I waved a hand.

"Go to bed, Desdemona. You need your sleep."

I stared at him, and then nodded. "All right. Wake me—"

"If I need to. I can manage it." He rolled his eyes.

I left then. There was no need for anything further, and at the mention of bed, my entire body seemed to droop. I slid off my shoes and pants and got into bed. Before I even hit the pillow, I was asleep.

I woke to shouting downstairs. A glance at the window told me it was dark outside, so I'd slept for a couple of hours. Holy hell. I didn't know what it was, but I fell out of bed and went running, pulling up spells in my head, feeling the magic tingle not only in my fingers, but my entire upper body.

I burst into the kitchen, hands out in front of me, and saw my sisters laughing.

"What in the name of blazes is going on here?" I shouted. "I thought we were under attack!"

Both of them, and Doc, I noticed, stared at me.

"Where are your pants?" Daniella asked.

I looked down. "Oh, shit," I said. "I didn't stop to think. I heard yelling, and I came running."

"You are really jumpy," Deirdre said.

"Had you been to Hell, you might understand why."

"I would have woken you had things gone awry," Doc chided.

"What is going on, since none of you can keep quiet?" I felt cross.

Daniella laughed. "I hate to admit when you're right, Desi, but you are right." She sighed. "Hey! Beeval! Where'd you guys go?"

I heard a response that had to be Beeval but I couldn't make it out. "Did he get out of the cupboard by himself?"

Doc nodded. "He did, and he came down here. I directed him to the fridge, and he managed without making a mess."

"Which is when Evil put in an appearance," Deirdre added.

"Oh, crap." Well, they hadn't killed him, and no one was yelling at me. So maybe Beeval hadn't eaten—

Beeval came in with Evil. *Wearing* Evil. On his head. Like a hat.

My mouth fell open. Daniella and Deirdre watched me, and laughed at my expression.

"They appear to have formed an understanding," Doc drawled.

Beeval stopped next to me, and leaned against my leg. "Desimo, feel better."

"You feel better?"

He looked up at me, and the fear and soul-crushing sadness I'd seen in his eyes wasn't as prominent. Some of that could possibly be attributed to the chicken on his head, but I liked to think Evil was only part of it.

"I better. I like feather bird," he added. One of his long arms reached up and patted Evil on the neck.

Evil clucked, and leaned into Beeval's hand, which was his way of showing approval for what was going on.

"And you were worried he'd eat him?" I gave Daniella the eye.

"I was, I admit it. I was wrong," Daniella conceded.

"I thought it was going to be a showdown," Deirdre said.

"Evil has to be the luckiest chicken I've ever seen," Doc said.

"So now that you know there's no fire, and no one is trying to kill us, how about you find some pants?" Deirdre asked. "Because if any of these things happen, you'll feel better if you have them."

"All right. Who's cooking?" I tossed over my shoulder as I went back upstairs. "Because I'm starving!" As I went upstairs, I checked the wards we'd placed around the house once I'd gotten back. They were still holding, as no one had attempted to cross them.

I hoped that Beeval was right, and that I had been a fun thing rather than a work thing for Ashlar, and thus not deserving of constant notice. Either that, or Ashlar had a ball busting boss. I didn't care—whatever kept him from knowing I was gone.

We had to find an angel sword. I didn't even know where to look, much less what I was looking for. I hoped like hell that Zane had found out something in his library. Which, once all this was over, if we all made it, I would need to check out.

Since he wasn't trying to raise zombies, or kill us, I supposed having a necromancer as a neighbor wasn't a bad thing. But I wasn't sure, so we'd need to wait and see.

And if we all made it out alive. That wasn't a sure thing. I got dressed, and went back downstairs. "Have you sorted dinner yet?" I asked Daniella.

"Deirdre called to the Saloon, and ordered all of our favorites. She'll be back shortly."

"Why do we fight again?" I asked with a smile as I got glasses out and poured tea.

"I don't know. We should enjoy this tonight. Tomorrow is the funeral," Daniella said.

"And the family descends," I added wryly.

"Oh, goddess. I almost forgot. What are we going to say to them? I've never even met them." Daniella looked worried.

I laughed. "With all that's going on, we're worried about how to talk to long-lost family."

"Have you met our family? We're all dangerous and mad as hatters. And they've obviously been fed a diet of the crazy Deadwood side."

"There is that," I agreed. "We'll need to talk to them, after we get through tomorrow. What did you plan?" I asked. "I'm sorry I couldn't—"

"No, you couldn't. You had to heal," Daniella said firmly. "There was no other choice."

"No other choice to what?" Deirdre came in, her arms full of bags. And good smells.

I just knew there was a crab and hollandaise burger for me in there. Hopefully the fries were still hot. "Gimme," I said. "That smells delicious."

Beeval came in, drawn by the smell. "Is time for eat?" he asked hopefully. Evil sat contentedly on his head.

"I brought extra, you know, just in case," Deirdre said.

A knock at the door stopped us all for a moment.

"Right on time," Daniella said. She went to the door and opened it.

Zane stood on the porch. "Am I interrupting?" he asked.

"No, we are having dinner, and you're invited," Deirdre said. "I've even gotten you a burger. Come in." She wheeled around and gave me a look.

"What?" I mouthed.

She widened her eyes as she walked back to the island where she'd left all the food.

Zane stopped. "Apparently, there was nothing to worry about."

I turned. He was watching Beeval and Evil. "No, somehow they worked it all out without any of us having to get involved."

"I don't even pretend to understand," Zane said, shaking his head. "But I'm glad. I'm already fond of Beeval."

"Well, it's you and me, then," I said with a smile.

"Hey, it's more than that," Daniella said. "He's growing on me."

Deirdre laughed. "You're all claiming love, but who brought the burgers? Beeval, I got you one, too."

I smiled gratefully at Deirdre. I knew it was madness to keep a demon in the house, but I couldn't abandon him. I knew that in my bones. It also seemed that losing Meema had quieted something within us—we hadn't fought at all since I'd crawled out of Hell. I hadn't even felt the urge, and normally, I wanted to kill one or both of them on a regular basis. It was gone, as though it had never been there.

Why? It was another one of those things we'd need to manage ... later.

Together, we sat around the island, eating the deliciousness from the Saloon No. 10 and talking and laughing, almost like a normal family. Three witches, a necromancer, a demon and his live chicken hat, and a ghost.

It could be worse.

CHAPTER TEN

I woke the next morning before sunrise. It wasn't much before, because I could see the streaks of light in the eastern sky from the windows in the hall.

Today was the day we buried Meema. Her coffin—which unfortunately did not contain her, but which Deirdre and Daniella had spelled at the funeral home—would lie next to Granny's.

Who was in her coffin, I supposed.

I showered, and dressed in a long black dress, pulling my hair back into a bun. Even though it was summer, and warm, I'd chosen a dress with a high neck and long sleeves. There was no need to sport my Hell marks—or as the town would see it, my new tats—at Meema's funeral. They didn't need any more to gawk at.

I went downstairs, the first one up. That meant I started the coffee. After I got the pot going, Doc appeared.

"I wish I could go with you," he said.

"She's not in there, Doc," I protested. "You know that."

He put his hands in his pockets. "I feel like I need to pay my respects."

"You're doing that right now."

"What do you mean?"

"By taking care of us," I said quietly, pulling food out of the fridge, not wanting to meet his eyes.

Silence, then, "Oh. Well, I do what I can."

I looked up. "I'm glad."

"So am I, darlin'," he said.

There was a knock on the door. "Well, here comes the rest of the family. You want to meet them?"

"I never fight unless I have to. I'll stand back and watch," he said with a smile.

"Coward," I replied as I walked to the door. Opening it, there were three women dressed all in black.

"Hello. I'm Desdemona," I said. "Are you the Deanas?"

The eldest one laughed. "Is that what you're calling us?"

"Isn't that what you all are named?" I asked. "And come in." I stood back from the door.

"This is Granny's house?" The woman who appeared to be in the middle in age looked around.

"It is," I said. "We had it moved off of Main Street a while back, and then redid it."

"I like the ceilings," said the youngest.

"Okay, so how do we refer to each of you?" I asked.

"I am DeAnna," said the eldest. "I changed my name after I had Dee," she touched her daughter's arm. "There's only one Deana."

"Well, that makes it easier."

"No, there's more than one," the youngest said. "I'm the only one who goes by Deana. Don't listen to them. They're not sure if they need to be bitter. They loved Auntie Desi."

"Shut up, Deana," said Dee.

"This is going to be a super reunion," I said. "Come in and have coffee, and we can continue the hostilities there." I turned my back on them.

There was whispering behind me, but I ignored it. It seemed the Deanas had the same sorts of problems we did. I grinned.

"The coffee's almost done, and we have all the fixings," I said as I got cups out. "Deirdre and Daniella will be down in a while."

"So where is he?" Deana, the youngest, asked.

"Who?" I turned around.

"Come on, don't 'who' me. Great-great-whatever-grandad. Doc Holliday. Gran told us all about him. Said he was a grumpy bastard."

"I am, when given reason.," Doc materialized. "The rest of the family?" he asked me.

I nodded. "DeAnna, your great-granddaughter. Dee, your great-great-granddaughter. And the one calling you a grumpy bastard is Deana. The great-great-great," I finished.

Doc had reappeared wearing a hat. He tipped it at the three of them. "Ladies, I am delighted to meet you."

None of them, even Deana, looked like they knew what to say.

"You're a lot more pleasant than Mom told us," DeAnna said.

"Well, I've undergone an attitude adjustment," Doc said. "It is possible, after a hundred years or so."

"What's the plan for today?" Dee asked.

"We're having the service, and then the burial. It's not planned, but people will come to the shop."

"So most of the day, then?" Deana asked.

I nodded. "Yes. How long are you staying for?"

DeAnna started to speak but Dee stopped her. "We're not sure," Dee said.

That was interesting. I poured four cups of coffee. There was silence as everyone fixed their drinks.

"What time is the funeral?" Deana asked.

I sighed. "Soon. As a matter of fact, I need to go upstairs and make sure everyone's up. Oh, if you see a chicken, he's a house chicken. If he's sitting on a short, weird guy...uh...well, that guy belongs here, too. I'll be right back." I ran lightly up the stairs.

"Did she say chicken?" one of them asked.

"Yes, indeed," Doc said. "We got all kinds here. The house chicken is Evil. The short, weird guy is a demon that followed Desdemona from Hell, and his name is Beeval. They are the best of friends." Doc's voice followed me up the stairs.

I knocked on Deirdre's door.

"I'm almost ready," she called.

"Excellent. Company's here," I said. I kept going to Daniella's room.

She came out the door as I reached her room. "They here?" she asked, tucking her hair up into a bun.

Seemed we had the same idea. "Yes."

"And?"

"It's interesting."

"What are they doing?"

"I left them with Doc," I admitted.

"Oh, that's going to be great. Jeez, Desi!" She hurried in front of me, banging on Deirdre's door. "Quit stalling, chicken! Come on!" Daniella hurried down the stairs, slowing as she reached the bottom.

"Coming, coming." Deirdre's voice was tired as she came out of her room. "Hey," she said to me. "How are they?"

"Annoyed. Don't really understand."

"Well, we have to make them understand, even if they don't want to be part of Deadwood," Deirdre said briefly. "This is stupid, and I'm annoyed that Deana didn't ever try to make things better."

"I think she did make things okay with Meema," I said, as we walked down the stairs together.

"Doesn't help us now," Deirdre muttered. She put a smile

on her face. "I'm so glad you could come," she said to the three women who watched us. "I wish we'd met under better circumstances."

"We loved Meema," DeAnna said.

"So did we," Daniella said.

"How much time before we have to leave?" Deana asked. "Because there's more than you told us about how she died."

"How do you know?" I asked with an overly casual shrug.

"Because you don't die," Dee said. "We know. Just because we aren't here doesn't mean we don't know."

"Yeah, well, since you're not here," I snapped, "you really don't know."

"So tell us," Deana said.

She seemed the least angry. But the anger wasn't helping anything. I should know, having lived with it for a hundred years or so.

"Why are you so angry with us?" Deirdre said. "I don't understand that. We've never done anything to you. Nothing. We wished Deana well, even though we missed her always." She looked at the three Deanas, her face earnest.

DeAnna glanced at Dee. Dee shrugged. Deana threw up her hands. "For God's sakes. This is so stupid." She glared at her mom and grandmom. "Why are you guys carrying on Gram's whatever? This isn't your baggage. Dump that shit. This is family that's still here."

"What did your mom say?" I asked DeAnna. "I mean, seriously. We weren't happy when she left, but we all got it— get it. None of us resented her, or stayed pissed. So what crawled up her butt?"

"A big stick." Deana glared at her elders. "Don't give me that look. Gram was mad she had to leave, but she didn't, did she?" She turned to me, and my sisters.

"No. She could have stayed here."

"And never died," DeAnna said.

Deirdre said, "You don't know that. We don't really know the deal with Granny's longevity. She did die, after all."

"And according to Meema, she chose that," I added.

"How do you choose it?" Deana asked.

"She just gave up and let her soul go," Doc said quietly.

"Yeah, look what her deal for immortality gave her," Deirdre grumped. She pointed at the Deanas. "That doesn't give you the right to say anything! We're the ones dealing with the fallout!"

"What fallout?" Dee asked.

"Well, you're about to deal with it, so save it if you want to bitch, because your turn is coming," Daniella added.

"Stop!" Deana yelled, holding up her hands. "There are too many people talking, and I can't keep all of you straight. It would great to have names that start with something other than 'D', but we don't, so I'm going to start with the basics. What deal did my three-times-great make that was such crap? What is she? Your ...?" She looked around with raised brows.

Deirdre looked at me. "Why don't you do the honors? You've sure as hell earned it."

Daniella nodded. "Go ahead, Desi."

I sighed. "Okay, this is what we know. Granny, Meema's mother, lived here in 1876. She fell in love with this guy." I jerked my thumb at Doc. "And in desperation, she went to a demon for help. Apparently her—our—family has some witch background, but we don't know how much. Granny didn't write much in her diaries about her family before she moved here. So anyway." I took a breath. "She makes a deal with a demon. Sells her and our mom's soul for power, immortality, and Doc."

"I was not aware of any of this," Doc said.

I held up a hand. "He rolled out, and Granny took his ghost after he died. He's been around ever since. Not always happily, which is understandable. During that time, Granny had to hand over two souls, and she talked two women with consumption into taking her and Meema's place. I know, right?" I could see the looks on the Deanas' faces. "Not cool. But she took all their kids, and gave them a home and money. Apparently, the souls hung on with the fake story until recently. And then the demon, named Ashlar, showed up here. He was pissed at being tricked. So he dragged me and Meema to Hell."

"Literal Hell?" DeAnna asked.

"Yes. I have the scars." I lowered my high collar, and pulled up my left sleeve.

Dee gasped.

"Ashlar put Meema in the River of Hell. I don't think there's any way to get her out of there." My voice caught, and I closed my eyes for a moment, thinking of poor Meema in that disgusting goo. "I barely got out myself. If it wasn't for Beeval, I'd probably still be there," I admitted.

"So we found Granny's diaries, and found out all this stuff. She screwed a lot of stuff up, which explains why she told us to be a force for good here in our little corner of the world," Deirdre said.

"And the demon Ashlar hasn't noticed that not only is Desi gone, but one of his little minions seems to have disappeared as well. We're on the lookout for that, just so you know," Daniella said.

"The minion?" Dee asked, her forehead creased.

"No, Ashlar, the pissed demon. He is going to come back. And he told us that he was coming for all of us. All the Nightingale women, was how he phrased it. You're part of this. I'm sorry."

No one spoke. It was a lot to take in. I knew it. I continued, "We have to kill the demon. There's no other way."

"Can't you just give him what he wants?" Deana asked.

"Well, he has Meema," Daniella said. "But Granny is gone, and he's never going to get her soul. It's not possible. So no, we can't."

"Granny screwed us all," DeAnna said. "Did my mom know that?"

I shook my head. "No. None of us knew until a couple of days ago."

"What do you need?" Dee asked.

Her mom whipped her head to glare at her, or reprimand her, but Dee ignored it.

"We can't leave Deadwood. Well, we can, but we begin to age, and at this point, I don't know what will happen. Like, will we look like the Cryptkeeper? I've driven west close to the border, but that wasn't very far. I think we need to go further." I'd been thinking about this.

"For what?" Deana asked.

Daniella answered her. "The only thing that we're sure can kill a demon. An angel sword."

CHAPTER ELEVEN

No one spoke after that. Then Deirdre looked at her watch. "Shit! We have to get going! The service starts in thirty minutes. We should already be there!"

A warning to Doc to keep an eye on things, and use the ghost gossip network if he needed to, and we piled into two cars, and went down to the church. St. John's Episcopal was where Meema had gone every Sunday, and Granny before her. Granny had also bought a section of ten plots for all of us in Mt. Moriah, thinking ahead that we'd all have to "die" from time to time. She'd even had an iron gate made for our section.

How could she be such a good planner in this, but such a shit planner in the bigger things, like making a deal with a crazy demon? Not that there were many who were sane. Although Beeval was. Or seemed to be.

We found parking, and walked to the church, tucked in between houses on Williams Street. It was filling up. Meema was believed to be the granddaughter of Granny, and the stigma of dance hall girl had finally faded. We were nice ladies who owned a tea and herb shop.

For the next two hours, we shook hands, hugged, introduced the Deanas, and then listened to a nice sermon for Meema. Then it was out to Mt. Moriah, and watching the coffin lower made all my tears come leaking out again.

Then they wouldn't stop. Dee leaned across and gave me a handful of tissues. I mopped at my face.

Meema was gone. I couldn't get my head around it, but this was final. Even though I knew she'd been gone since we'd gone to Hell, this was final. Real. What were we going to do without her? We had no plans because we'd never planned on her being gone.

I'd always figured if she wanted to go, we'd all talk about it, and then make plans from there. Not like this. Not by someone else's choice.

"We still have to get through the shop," Deirdre whispered in my ear, putting an arm around my waist.

"Jesus," I whispered back. "I don't know if I can."

"You can." Daniella came up on the other side of me. We stood together, the Nightingale girls, girls no longer.

Then Deana, and Dee, and DeAnna came and stood with us. "We're here with you. This is some screwed up shit, but we're here," Dee said quietly.

I reached across Daniella and squeezed her hand. "Thank you."

As I looked around, I saw the townspeople watching us. I could feel their approval. They liked seeing all of us, knowing that there were Nightingale women still there. We were a founding family. I tuned them out, because I needed to focus on getting through this, and then all the people who would come to the shop.

The shop was packed. Everyone had known and loved Meema, even the people on the Historical Society she'd gone hammer and tongs with when she'd wanted to move our house. We lived too close to the shop, and she wanted some privacy for us. Otherwise, people thought they could come to the door, seeing us during non-business hours. Plus, with Sturgis every year, she didn't want to be on Main Street anymore all day. Not that she didn't love the bikers, but it was nice to head up to Pearl Street and leave all the noise behind each day.

People brought food, because that's what they did. Deirdre and Daniella had been down here the day before and set up lots of teapots in readiness for today. They got them going with super speed.

"What can we do?" DeAnna asked.

"Get the tea going, and corral the food," I whispered back.

I'd say this for the Deanas: For all the carrying on earlier that morning, they went into efficiency mode, and were fantastic hostesses. It gave me hope, kind of like the new relationship I'd found with my sisters and Doc.

I clasped hands, accepted hugs, and listened to stories, and cried with the people of Deadwood; our neighbors and friends. By four o'clock, the last of the stragglers were leaving. We'd been taking shifts of cleaning up.

Zane had come to the church, the graveyard, and the shop, and he approached me. "What can I do?" he asked.

"Let's get this cleaned up, and get home."

He nodded, and the next time I saw him, he had a trash can, picking up all the paper cups. He was worming his way into my good graces whether I wanted him to or not. I wasn't sure anymore that I wanted to keep him out of said graces.

Finally, the shop was clean, and we walked out together, Daniella locking the door behind us. The entire day felt surreal, and my first thought turning onto Pearl Street was that I needed to tell Meema how nicely it had gone in the shop today.

But I couldn't. Meema wasn't there, and wouldn't be ever again. The tears fell again. "Oh, God," I whispered. We all walked into the kitchen, and everyone dropped into a chair, either at the island, or around the large table, where Granny's diaries were still spread out from our reading the night before. I sat at the table, and put my head down.

I must have fallen asleep, because when I sat up, my cheek felt sticky, and the imprint of my wrist was on the side of my cheek.

"Here, have some tea," DeAnna said, sliding a cup next to me.

"Thank you," I said.

She smiled, a small, sad smile. "I was so busy being aggravated that I forgot you girls were burying your mother. You might be way older than me, and my auntie, but today, you buried your mom. And I'm sorry, honey," she added. She patted my shoulder, not waiting for an answer, and walked away.

I could see all the Deanas were in the kitchen, with my sisters perched at the island, drinks in hand. Zane and Doc leaned against the counter out of the way of the Deanas, and to complete the family picture, Beeval came in with Evil on his head.

Beeval looked us all over and veered toward me. "Desimo. Feel better?"

He still smelled like brimstone and ass. But when he reached up to pat my arm with one of his long arms, I let him. I even leaned close, getting a face full of Evil feathers for my trouble. Evil clucked, and pecked at my head.

"I do now," I said.

Beeval patted me again, and then moved back to the kitchen. "Bacon?" he asked hopefully.

The Deanas turned around.

"What is that?" Dee asked.

"That's the demon with the chicken hat," Doc said, and he was trying not to laugh. "Welcome to Pearl Street."

"Is the chicken alive?" Deana asked.

"Yes," Daniella said.

"There is a story here, isn't there?" DeAnna asked.

Deirdre told the Evil story, and then added on the Beeval story.

"Bacon?" Beeval asked again, hearing his name.

"There's some in the lower drawer in the fridge," I said, getting up, feeling more than one hundred years old. I took my tea with me.

"Okay, so let's get back to our earlier conversation. If that's all right," Deana said. "What do you need from us?"

"We haven't talked about this," DeAnna said, not even turning around from the stove.

"Mom, if a demon is after Nightingale women, we don't need to talk about it. We're Nightingales," Dee said.

"Not that anyone else knows," DeAnna said. "We go by Holliday."

"You do?" Doc asked, the corners of his mouth turning up. "Well, isn't that a treat."

"Mom didn't know what else to use. She always said you were a fourth cousin," DeAnna said.

"You think the demon can't find us? I'd rather try and stop him than be worried about him," Deana said.

"We need your help," I said, stopping the arguing. I knew what women in the middle of an argument that wouldn't end soon sounded like. "We can't leave for long. Zane, what did you find out about angel swords? Please tell me you found something," I added.

Dee added a pan to the stove, putting bacon strips in it. Beeval hopped excitedly near her.

"The whole thing?" Dee asked to the room at large.

"Probably a good idea," Deirdre said. "Desi is right. We need you. And I'm hoping like hell you found something," she added to Zane.

"I did, but I'm not sure it's good news." Zane spoke quietly.

I felt the weight of his words like a bomb. Part of me felt like we'd just wasted a day. As much as I wanted to curl up and cry, that wasn't going to happen until the demon was stopped. We were on a ticking clock. I forced myself to take a breath. We needed to live, to make Meema's sacrifice worth it.

"It's okay," Daniella said. "We're used to less than great news."

"There's one angel sword that I think we have a chance of. I found a list of them in one of my books. And I've seen this one. I can get the book if you want to see it," he added.

"No," I waved my hand. "Give us the overview."

"We're going to have see a necromancer." He grimaced. "And one that's not very nice. In fact, he's kind of a big jackass. But he's the only one who has it."

"That's listed in the book?" Deirdre asked, disbelief all over her face.

"No. There are pictures of the swords, and I have seen this in his collection."

"Shit. Does he know what he has?" I jumped in.

Zane shook his head. "But the minute we go there, and try to buy it or barter for it, he'll know it's important to someone, and he's going to be a royal pain to deal with."

"Nothing like going uphill both ways, right?" Daniella said to me with a half-grin. "Wouldn't feel right otherwise."

"No, that tends to be our luck," I said.

Zane looked like he wanted to say something, then thought the better of it. He crossed his arms, and leaned back.

"What?" I asked. "Don't hold back."

"It's not a big deal. I'm just going over all the things I know about Gareth, and I decided it didn't matter. He's going to be a nightmare. That's all we need to know."

"Where is Gareth?"

"Vermont," Zane said with a frown.

"Oh, so somewhere totally close, then."

"How do we get it from him?"

"We're going to need to barter." Zane said. "He's more of the kind of stereotypical necromancer. You know, the kind you thought I was?" That was directed at me.

"Well, what does he like?"

Zane held his head in his hand, clearly not wanting to say. But he said it anyway. "Grave dirt."

"Oh, for goddess's sake," I said.

Daniella started to laugh. "How in the hell did this guy get an angel sword?"

"Honestly? He probably found it or stole it. Or bartered with someone who stole it." Zane looked embarrassed.

"Aren't angel swords kind of, I don't know, rare?" Deana asked. "How do you lose that kind of thing?"

"You'd be surprised," I said. "If people don't know what something is, they don't put any value on it. So?" I looked at Zane. "We have grave dirt. It's a staple for people who think we're more than herbalists and tea shop owners."

"Well, you are," Dee said. "Good to know you have what the weirdo will need."

"I need one of you to be a collector. He'll believe that," Zane added. "You might be good at this, Dee."

"This could be fun. Is he dangerous?"

"Mom! Really?" Deana asked.

"Well, it's a legitimate question!"

"He's a little nutty, to be honest. But he's not very skilled at any real magic. His talent is finding things, although he can't see that."

"It sounds kind of sad," Deirdre said.

Zane nodded. "It is. You'll need to give him a lot of grave dirt, so I don't feel bad. Where'd you get it, by the way? He'll want to know."

"Tell him it's from Deadwood. We collected it when the graveyards were moved, and not all the bodies made the move."

"Is that verifiable?" Zane asked.

"What, he checks?"

"Yes. I told you, he loves the stuff."

"You know some odd characters," Doc chimed in.

"Says the ghost," DeAnna added. "Everyone ready for something to eat?"

She'd pulled together food from all the leftovers we had from the shop, and made eggs and hash browns as well. It sounded crazy, but food was exactly what we needed right now.

Everyone grabbed a plate, and conversation ended. The only sound in the kitchen were the interesting sounds Beeval made eating his bacon, some clucking from Evil, and the clink of silverware on plates.

"That was perfect, DeAnna," Daniella said, pushing her clean plate away.

"Yeah, it was."

"You don't stop the mom things," DeAnna said. Then her face showed horror as she registered what she'd just said. "Oh, Lord, I have the biggest feet that I put into my mouth on the regular. I am so sorry."

"It's all right," Deirdre said. Her face was soft, softer than I'd seen it in a long time.

"So, when do we head out to visit grave dirt guy?" Deana asked.

"You want to go?" I asked. "We can't, so it has to be one of you."

She nodded.

"Zane, is there any other way to kill this bastard?" I asked.

He shook his head. "No. That's it."

I scrubbed at my hair with both hands, ruining the bun. "If we could just...wait." I stopped, staring off into the distance. "Zane, can I go do some reading in your library?"

He started, and then looked uncomfortable. "Yes, but..."

"But what?" I asked.

Everyone stared.

"I need to show you how it's organized."

"Okay. No biggie. We get it. You like your stuff the way you like it."

"What are you looking for?"

"I'm about to step right into your alley. Raising the dead," I said with a grin.

CHAPTER TWELVE

That night, Zane took me over and showed me his library in the basement of his little house. It was packed, and it was organized. He went over his system three times, which was done by date. It was obsessive, but with this big of a library, I could understand.

Then it was time to get Deana and Zane on the road to Vermont.

I nearly died when Deana asked if we couldn't just portal or something.

"It doesn't work that way," Daniella said kindly. "It would be nice if it did."

Deirdre booked them a hotel, a flight, and sent a huge box of grave dirt via UPS to the hotel. I wasn't kidding when I said we had some. All the moving of cemeteries here had caused a lot of dirt to be grave dirt—and Meema had suggested we collect as much as possible. That's what we kept in *our* basement. Along with the supplies for spells, and the bits needed for the kinds of potions the townspeople would ask us for. We were set for an apocalypse, materials-wise. But back to getting the angel sword. All they had to do was make the deal, and get the sword. They should be able to do it in a couple of days. We were already three days in, so if we got a week, we'd be lucky.

And while they were gone, I'd be working on the backup plan. Zane, to his credit, didn't ask me for details on why I was looking in his library to raise the dead. Not the actual dead, like he used to, or whatever. But the spirit of someone dead. He was a restful research helper. He just showed me where to look, and told me to text him if I had any questions.

"You might save the actual raising for when I get back," he said as we walked back to our house. On the way, Mrs. Kittrick came to her gate. "I'm sorry about your mother," she said. "She and I weren't close, but she was a good woman."

I had to stop myself from staring. "Thank you," I stammered. "We miss her."

"I'm sure you do. I wanted to let you know." She whirled around and shuffled back to her house.

"I thought she hated you," Zane whispered.

"She does," I whispered back.

"The dead are all saints," he responded. "So no one feels like they can speak badly. She looks like she comes from that generation."

"You need to tell me what the cats say," I said. "Later."

Zane stared for a moment, then laughed. "It took me a sec to figure out what you were talking about."

"When did you learn to talk to animals?"

He shrugged. There was something about him that told me he was reluctant to talk about his past, his learning, his history. A slight warning bell sounded in my head.

I brushed it off. He'd been nothing but helpful, and nice to all of us. Were he a typical necromancer, he'd have already killed the cats, and crossed us. They were generally a selfish bunch. From what he'd said, he came from that background, but made a change. I wondered why.

Then I decided it didn't matter. His actions spoke for him,

and his actions said he was a decent man, with honor, and principles. I'd leave it at that until I had a reason to think otherwise. I'd been right about Beeval. I just hoped I'd never see a reason to be wrong about Zane.

"I told you, I trained with a witch. We... discovered that being able to communicate with animals was a gift."

"You're going to have to tell me what Evil thinks," I said.

"I don't get a whole lot going on there. I'm sorry," he added quickly. "I know you all love him. But... he's a chicken who was partially dead."

I laughed then. "That's true. But what is there is harmless, and sweet."

"He likes Beeval."

"You think? Jeez, it's like an instant bromance with those two."

"Better than Beeval trying to eat him."

"Bacon is better than chicken, apparently." Which reminded me we needed more bacon. We might have to find someone to buy from directly in the amounts that Beeval ate. "Moving along, thank you for letting me look into your library."

"Who are you raising from the dead?" His curiosity had finally gotten the better of him.

I was impressed. "I don't know if it's possible, but I want to see."

"You know, that is kind of my forte. You know, my job. I could help you with it." He gave me a look.

I took a deep breath before speaking. "It feels like a long shot, and maybe sort of stupid."

"There is no stupid when you're looking for ways to take down a demon."

"Is it possible to find Granny's soul?"

"Why?"

"We've read the diaries, well, part of them," I amended, because we certainly hadn't read all of them, "And I feel like there's more she's not telling us. Like we're missing something. I could be wrong, but I listen to my gut, and that's what it's telling me."

He frowned as we walked back into our house. "I don't know. How long has she been dead?"

"Over one hundred years. And she chose her death. Which is weird, too, because neither Doc nor Meema ever talked about how she died, and we're not supposed to be able to die. Jeez! This family! The secrets are going to kill us all!"

Zane patted my arm. "No, they're not. There are a lot of them, all seeming to stem from your grandmother. Maybe," he hesitated.

"What?"

"Maybe we need to press Doc. I get that there's a détente going on, but maybe he knows more than he's telling. He did spend twenty-plus years cooped up in her room."

"Good point. I hate to ruin things—everything is so pleasant right now—but we might need to." I tapped my finger on my lips, thinking. "Hey, do you think that necromancer will give up the sword without a huge fight?"

"If you take Dee, and she acts like a collector—he's a collector himself. He'll understand the drive. He can't think that she's interested in the magic. It's a magic object, not made of this earth, and it's rare. That's her focus."

"Well, you're going with her. You'll be able to manage that, won't you?"

He nodded, but looked concerned. "It makes me nervous that you're thinking of trying to contact the spirit of your grandmother. It's not really raising the dead, per se, which I'm glad of. That takes skill, despite what you might think."

I decided I might as well go for the gold in uncomfortable topics. "Do I need to apologize for thinking the worst of you when we met?"

He shook his head. "No. Gareth is like many necromancers.

I know that I'm considered slightly odd by most and someone to avoid. I need to thank you for not killing me."

"It was close." I smiled.

"I prefer to keep on living, so thank you. Anyway, let me get packed, and we'll get this going." He took a moment to speak with Dee and Deana, and then with a wave, went back to his place.

Deirdre, Daniella, the Deanas and I all sat around the dining room table that night, drinking tea and telling stories. It was nice. The feeling of hostility had dissipated, although I could tell that DeAnna was nervous about her daughter and granddaughter heading off with Zane. She managed it for a bit, but finally, the nervousness won out.

"Do you think they're going to be all right?" She nodded at her offspring. "I can't seem to calm my worry."

I believed in gut feelings. "What do you think will happen?" I asked.

Deirdre and Daniella looked over, letting the other conversation lapse. They knew the tone in my voice.

"That's he's a weasel, he'll try to trap them, or something," DeAnna said. "I don't know, and I feel stupid for worrying about something I can't name, but I can't stop!" She wrung her hands, the frown making her forehead wrinkle.

I looked at my sisters, a question in my eyes. They nodded. Turning back to DeAnna, I asked, "Have you ever done any magic? Did your mother teach you anything?" I kept my voice neutral. I thought I knew the answer, and if I was right, Deana —our sister—needed a serious bitch slap.

DeAnna shook her head. "No. Momma didn't want us to be involved in anything that she was growing up."

"I loved Deana, and I miss her all the time, but if she were here, I'd smack the crap out of her," Deirdre said. "I understand not wanting you all to grow up like she did but you can't change who you are. Had she prepped you, even a little, you'd be in better shape for this."

"What, you think we're going to lose?" Deana asked.

"No, I don't. But I think this is going to be tough. We've grown up and been using magic our entire lives. It's comfortable for us, even when it's difficult. You guys don't have that knowledge base, or any kind of comfort. And Deana should have known better."

"Then what are we waiting for? What can you show us now?" Dee asked.

"Not a lot," Daniella said. "But we can give the two of you protection spells, that you can cast easily. And slowing spells. So if someone comes at you, you can slow them down. Maybe one more?" She looked between me and Deirdre.

"Fire," Deirdre said. "Catch someone on fire, they leave you be fast. It'll give you enough time to get away."

"That's pretty tough," I objected. "Come on, I just got fire from Hell, and I don't even get that one yet."

"No, just like a cherry bomb kind of thing. Something they can throw, and activate with a word."

I nodded. "Something that looks like tea bags, so you can easily take it on the plane."

"It's not going to blow up mid-air is it?" DeAnna was alarmed.

"No, it needs the spoken word to set it off. We don't want anyone blowing parts off," Daniella laughed. "Well, come on ladies. You're not going to get much sleep tonight. But you'll leave here feeling better, and a little more safe. And that's the important thing."

Together we all trooped down to the basement. Beeval came through, with Evil sleeping on his head. Our basement, which was in the shape of a long rectangle, was set up like one big herbal dispensary. A long work bench was built along one wall, with room for five people to work, and spread out. There were mortars and pestles, because some things had to be ground by hand. The other three walls were taken up with large and small glass jars, holding all manner of herbs. The far end of the basement had drying racks for the herbs that needed drying before they were stores. Some didn't. But we took our herbals seriously. They'd saved our asses more than once.

Nothing like this, and I hoped our dedication would pay off. First things first. Set our newbies up with the things they needed. Deirdre took on making fire, and she pulled Deana to her. Daniella was better with the protection aspect, so she began to gather the materials for the spell, towing Dee next to her.

I started taking down the jars with the herbs for a slowing spell. "Come on, DeAnna. We're going to make a slowdown teabag."

She gazed at me doubtfully. "Will this work?"

I nodded. "Yes. We're going to make these so that they're like beginner spells. All Dee or Deana will need to do is speak the spell word, and it will activate the spell. As you get better with magic, you won't need the herbs. But they are a focus, and a helper, until you get to that place."

"Why wouldn't Momma have wanted us to know this? She told me her whole life how glad she was to get out of Deadwood, and I came here with that in mind. But ..." She looked at me, and the confusion in her expression was almost heartbreaking. "I haven't seen that you three are bad. I mean, you did drag us into your mess. But it's our mess, too, isn't it? Because we're all the children of the original Desdemona?"

I put my arm around her. It had to be difficult to learn that what you'd been taught your entire life was not only not accurate, it also wasn't the big bad wolf you'd been told it was. "We're family. You are helping out family. When this is over, we'll teach you anything you want. Anything at all. You can stay here and learn, whatever you want. I promise."

DeAnna surprised me with a hug. "Thank you. Thank you for giving us a chance when we came in not ready to do the same."

"You're welcome. Time to focus." I nodded at the jars on the long workbench. St. John's wort, hyssop, sage, and a quartz stone tied into a teabag. We mixed up the ingredients in silence. The slowdown spell was not overly difficult: Agrimony, angelica root, ash prickly bark. If you were feeling frisky, you could also add some bladder wrack, buchu, or lemongrass. I added all three. I felt extremely frisky.

"This is it?" DeAnna asked. "It seems so simple."

"It is." I nodded. "The herbs are there to help with focus, to protect the user against whatever harm is aimed at them. We charge these before you can use them, which means we put magic in them. When the word is used to activate, the herbs allow the user to cast magic. It's perfect when you're just beginning. But you need to be with a trustworthy witch—one with less than positive intentions can hurt a beginning magical user."

"Good thing you're trustworthy. How many do we need to make?"

"Oh, maybe twenty, twenty-five. I want you to each have five teabags of each—did you hear that?" I raised my voice so that my sisters heard. "Make twenty-five each so that they can practice?"

"We're going to do them here, in front of you?" DeAnna was definitely nervous.

"Yes, so we can help you be as efficient as possible." I didn't look up as I spoke. I'd figured out that DeAnna had a hard time with the woo-woo aspect of magic, and I needed to keep things as level as possible, with logic and reason.

I literally would have smacked Deana back into the hereafter if she were with us right now. She'd hurt her offspring by not at least making them familiar with aspects of magic. And given DeAnna, at least, a complex.

It took us longer than normal, because we were going slow to show them what we were doing, and how, but finally, we had all the bags assembled.

"Who wants to go first?" I asked with a grin. "School is now in session!"

CHAPTER THIRTEEN

We saw Dee, Deana, and Zane off the next morning. I felt good, even slightly hopeful, as we watched them drive away in Zane's Land Rover.

The impromptu teaching last night—well, this morning—had gone well. Even DeAnna, who was by far the most nervous of the three, had done well, and managed to set off all the spells. They'd been alarmed when Deirdre, Daniella and I took turns being the target. But it had become fun when Daniella said, "Listen, if we can't dodge stuff from you guys, we deserve to get knocked on our asses. So hit us with your best. We can take it. Seriously. We used to practice with Granny and Meema. The goal is to *not* get knocked on your ass."

They'd relaxed then, and Deana showed signs of being really proficient. I debated whether or not to invite her alone, and then decided against it. If they wanted to learn, they could come and spend the summer here, and come back whenever they wanted.

Like a mother ship.

"I hope they're back fast," DeAnna muttered.

"Well, don't hope too hard. You're going to learn while they're gone." I put an arm around her and gave her a squeeze.

"Learn what?" Her eyebrows went up.

"First, we're going to go over to Zane's and see if we can call Granny's spirit back."

"Not Meema?"

I could feel my face fall. "No. She's not in a place where we can reach her."

"I'm sorry," DeAnna said quietly. "I know how hard it is to lose her."

I nodded, feeling the tears. Then I sniffed, and swiped at my face. "Well, that's neither here or there right now. Right now, we need to see if we can find Granny and shake the damn truth out of her."

"She might not want to tell us."

"No." I remembered my conversation with Zane last night, "But before we do that, we need some other information." I caught Daniella's eye, and jerked my head.

She saw it, and nudged Deirdre. That was the great thing about being with your sisters all the time—there wasn't always a need for words.

DeAnna trailed behind us, arms crossed.

"Doc!" I yelled. "Come on, we need to talk!"

He drifted through a wall. "I was called by the dulcet tones?"

"Yes. You were. Prepare to be uncomfortable."

"That does not bode well," he said.

"It's time for truth. Like, all the truth."

"In what respect, darlin'? I've been as honest as I could be."

"We need to know more about the time you spent with Granny."

A cloud passed over his face, which was weird, being able to see this on a ghost. But there had definitely been a cloud. "What?" I asked.

"That was a bad time for me, Desdemona. I'll try and remember things, but now, it seems like a dark blur. I was angry, very angry. So was Desi. Neither of us were at our best," he finished.

"Yeah, I know. But I need to know about how and why she died."

"Why?"

Oh, he was hiding something. I could just tell. It was all over him. Next to me, DeAnna sat down at one of the chairs at the island.

"Because it's weird, don't you think? She does this deal, and gets to live forever—"

"Without being arrogant, I believe she had plans to live with me," Doc said softly.

"What happened with that?" DeAnna interrupted.

Normally, I would have verbally slapped her, but if she helped Doc be more comfortable, this would be better for me. For all of us. The secrets had to end.

"I was dying. From the time I moved from Texas, I knew I was on borrowed time. I was always grateful that women were willing to be with me, but I had nothing to offer a woman. Desi did try to tell me that she could help me, but I was resigned and cynical at that point. I didn't listen. Once I went south again, and met Kate..." He shrugged. "It was all over then in regards to other women. And I? I was dying, and Kate was willing to take on caring for me, in many ways. I could not have come back to Desi even had I wanted to."

"Easier that way?" Deirdre commented.

"I was no saint, darlin,'" Doc said with a wry expression. "I did care for Desi. As I told you, she was a great deal of fun, and I enjoyed our time together. That was the most I could give a woman in that time. Once she brought me here, I was angry."

"How long did you fight?" I asked.

"Until she died. I didn't know she was planning it."

"What? She planned her own death?" DeAnna was shocked.

"Yes. If you were to live here, from my understanding, you would possibly not die."

"I don't know," I said. "I wish we knew more about Granny's family. In order for us to all have the amount of power we do, there had to be something there to begin with. No demon gives this much power."

"Why not?" asked DeAnna.

"Because while they say they want to help you, demons are like everyone else. They're looking out for their interests. And their interests are getting souls to Hell, to work for them. I don't really know, but that's the impression I got. The main point is, you don't do deals with demons. And Granny did—out of desperation, I guess. But she had to have some talent for the craft to be going on with. She managed to keep this town on the rails, and most of the supernatural shitheads out of it. She taught Meema to do the same, and then Meema taught us. That's not just a demon gift." I nodded at Doc.

He pursed his lips, thinking. "I know that about five years before she died, she cried almost every night."

"Why?" Daniella beat me to it.

This was more like it.

"I don't know. By that time, I wasn't so almighty angry, and listening to a woman cry is no one's idea of a good time. Whatever it was, it was a deep hurt."

"So why did she choose to die?" Deirdre had a fierce look on her face.

"Right before she died, she called to me, and I came, but grudgingly. She told me that she was sorry, that she didn't know how to let me go, and she'd missed me so much after I left. I told her that I wanted to be free. She said she was sorry, and looked down at her hands. They were in her lap, palms upturned. Then she got up and walked out of the room. That was the last time I saw her, or spoke to her, so it must have been a few days before she died. I rather think she took something," he added. "She was drinking a tea before bed. Your mother found her the next morning. I did come in to observe the screaming." He crossed his arms.

"Okay, so she killed herself. She was ready to go. But why? This just doesn't make sense. Meema was young, only in her late thirties, and we were little, like nine or ten. Granny was so invested in taking care of Deadwood—why kill herself?" I shook my head.

"Something changed," DeAnna said.

"Like what?" I wondered.

"Something she thought was one way, and it changed."

"But she'd already sent the two consumptive women off with Ashlar. I don't think he's known since then. He didn't seem the type to sit back and wait quietly for the right time." Daniella looked at Doc for confirmation.

He nodded slowly. "I would agree. He had the anger of just learning he'd been taken."

"Exactly," I said. "Patience wouldn't seem like one of his virtues—unless he's having us on."

"No," Doc said. "That was an angry demon who just heard the bad news."

"Okay, so we will assume it wasn't the demon, although that's not a for sure thing," I said, holding up a finger. "So what could have changed?"

"Well, maybe the terms of the bargain she made? Something she'd thought about herself that turned out not to be true? Or something that was true, that she'd never thought of?" Daniella asked.

I laughed. "Did you ever talk to her?" I asked DeAnna.

"No, but I'm trying to think of my mother, who sounds a lot like Granny. Secretive, personal obsessions, a very fixed point of view—she'd be rolling in her grave if she knew what we were up to."

"I wish I knew why your mom was so against all of us here. We loved her. She was our sister. I don't get that either." Deirdre had lost the fierce look.

"Secrets become bigger and bigger with every person that carries them," Doc observed.

"Well, thank you, scholar Doc Holliday!" I threw up my hands. "That solves everything!"

He shrugged. "I always knew there were secrets. I thought most of them were with Desi. But maybe there were more?"

"We need to talk to her spirit, if we can." I was thinking about the books Zane had showed me, going over where to begin.

"Even if we do, do you think she'd tell us?" DeAnna asked. "It sounds like she took a great deal of them with her, and she did it on purpose."

"True, but maybe the outcomes of all her shit will loosen her tongue," I said. "If not, there's always the massive guilt trip. I think she did have some," I added for Doc's benefit.

"I think she did as well," he agreed. "That didn't comfort me at the time."

I laughed at his tone. "It's amazing to me how your spirit still manages the best sarcasm in the house."

"It's a gift, darlin'."

"Well, we could beat more info out of you, but I don't know that it would be productive, so I suppose I'll table that to go and rummage in Zane's library. We'll have to be neat, actually," I said to DeAnna. "The guy is worse with his books than we are with our stillroom."

"I can understand that. We'll be careful," she promised.

"Doc, if you think of anything, will you let me know when we get back? If we can find Granny's spirit, which is starting to feel like a bigger undertaking than even I thought, we need to know exactly what we want to ask her."

He nodded, and drifted toward the door of the kitchen. Then he was gone.

"I'm going to the store. We're out of bacon. We also need to open tomorrow, God help us all. Because that's just what we need, but we need to." Daniella sighed.

"I'm going to make sure we have everything we might need," Deirdre said. "I'll be in the stillroom if you need me."

"Don't go all crazy ordering stuff," Daniella cautioned. "If we're out of something, call me first, okay? No Amazon!"

"Okay, okay, I promise," Deirdre said. "Love you."

"Love you," we both said automatically.

Deirdre smiled and walked from the kitchen and I heard her going downstairs a moment later.

Daniella sighed, hugged me and DeAnna, and also left.

"Ready?" I asked DeAnna.

"You three are very efficient," she said.

"We have to be. It's usually quiet and low-key here. But when things go bad, it's in a hurry and all at once. We never have a build-up to doom or anything like that."

She nodded, and we left for Zane's house. I hoped we'd find what we needed. This was not really my forte. Everyone thinks witches can talk to the dead, but as a rule, we don't want much to do with the dead. Our responsibility was to the living. Dead folks, whether body or spirit, are just not in our wheelhouse. I didn't mention it to DeAnna, but if we couldn't get Granny on the afterlife horn, I was going to try and call my sister's spirit back. Better to keep that one to myself, though.

Enter the necromancers. As we moved into Zane's library, I took the time to marvel at his books. This was a lifetime of dedication to collecting. He had hundreds of of them. But he'd pulled out twenty or so that he thought would help. Probably didn't want my hands touching more of them than I had to, I thought with a grin.

"Grab one from the stack on the table," I said. "Zane already got these ready for us, probably so we didn't dig around in his system too much."

"Saves us the trouble," DeAnna said. "Never look that sort of gift horse in the mouth."

We both started to read, and I saw that Zane had thoughtfully left pads of paper and pens for note taking.

Why did he have to be so thoughtful? At this point, he was going to have me inviting necromancers to tea.

He's not a par for the course kind of guy, I told myself. Simmer down.

Three books in, I found something I thought might work. It was dark magic, darker than we preferred to dabble in. We'd had witches come through that wanted to partner up, do some big thing they were planning, but Meema had always declined. Her attitude was that we had quite enough to do with keeping the crazy out of Deadwood.

While we weren't Sturgis, that yearly gathering brought all sorts through town. And there were some like us, some with magical skills and supernatural interests. We didn't sleep a lot during Sturgis.

"I think I have something," I told DeAnna. "But I'm not sure. Take a look and see what you think." I slid the book across to her.

"You think I might have an opinion on this?" Her eyebrows went up into her bangs. "I think you're giving me more credit than I deserve."

"We need to call a spirit that's been gone for over one hundred years. We need to figure out how to find that specific spirit, and then coax it here, if it even wants to be. I don't want to drag her here kicking and screaming, but I will if I have to. And yes, I think you have an opinion."

She read what I'd been reading. Then she looked up at me. "This might be it."

"Why don't we tidy this up, and take our notes and this book back with us? I can't copy all these pages, and be sure of getting it right," I said.

She nodded, and we stacked up all the preciouses, keeping out the one that might have the answer. Then we locked up Zane's house.

"They should be back tomorrow, right?" DeAnna asked.

"Yes, as long as Gareth isn't too difficult. But maybe a text is in order?" I could tell she was really worrying. "Zane's not going to let anything happen to them."

"You haven't known him very long, though, have you?" she asked as she gave me a sideways glance.

"No, but if he was going to screw us, he's had plenty of chances. Trust me. If he's bad, it will come out. But he has surprised me every time, so I am going to give him the benefit of the doubt."

"With my girls," DeAnna said.

"If this goes sideways, we die," I said. "It's not just your girls. It's all of us. All the Nightingale women. Is that not sinking in? Yes, you're helping us accomplish something that needs to be accomplished. But this isn't empty kindness on your part. We go down, you go down."

"You don't know that," she argued.

"No, I don't. You want to gamble and hope for the best with a demon? One that dragged me and Meema off like it was nothing? And threw Meema into suffering forever? Really? That's what you want to gamble with?"

We'd reached the house, and I stopped right before the porch, one hand holding the book, and the other on my hip. "DeAnna, we need you to be all in on this. This is not us using you, or something selfish. We're trying to save us all."

She stared back at me, and I couldn't tell what she was

thinking. Finally, she sighed. "I know this. I know it, but at the same time, I hear Momma in my head, muttering, 'That damn Deadwood,' and then she'd go off cussing. Something else happened, and I can't shake it."

"I'll agree with you there. For all that Doc told us, there's something more. But that's what we're doing. It sounds like," I added as we walked into the house, "your mom knew something that none of us knew. Maybe that's it." I stopped. "Maybe that's why she left? Holy shit," I breathed. "That's it, isn't it? She found out something, and that's what made her want to leave."

I set the book down on the dining table and sat myself down as well to consider this. I don't know why I'd never thought of it. Probably because Meema always supported Deana, and didn't make it a big negative drama thing, we never thought anything of it.

But if Deana had discovered something—something that was so bad, or scared her, or pissed her off—she would have left. None of us were ever what you'd call shy and retiring, or accepting of shit merely because we ought to be. We called a shit sandwich a shit sandwich, and never, ever asked for seconds.

"What do you think it was?"

"DeAnna, you have to try and remember all that your mom ever told you. I'll get you a notepad, and just start writing down the things she told you, anything you remember." I got up and hurried into the kitchen, leaving DeAnna staring after me. When I came back, she hadn't moved.

"Here, sit down, and close your eyes, and just let your memory go back. There's no pressure, no right or wrong, just anything you can remember, okay?"

"You might not like it," she warned.

"A little hurt feelings is way better than a lot dead," I said. I got her situated and left her staring out the front window while I went down to see Deirdre.

CHAPTER FOURTEEN

When I walked into the stillroom, I breathed in. Even now, in a time of crisis, walking in here and smelling all the herbs both calmed and soothed me. It balanced me.

"Hey," Deirdre said. "What's up?" She had glass jars around her, and was making more of what looked like the teabags we'd armed Dee and Deana with.

"I've got a direction, at least," I said. "And DeAnna is trying to remember what the hell might have happened with Deana."

"I think her idea that something changed, either for Granny or whatever, has legs."

"Yeah, but Deana left years after Granny died."

Deirdre shrugged. "I don't know. I can't believe what a head-case Granny was, and I'm having a hard time being anything but pissed because we're on serious clean-up duty from whatever the hell she put in motion."

"I think DeAnna has a decent idea."

Deirdre looked at me, not understanding.

"That Granny gave it up because she found out something that just took her will to live."

"Okay, I could see that. But what? I mean, making a deal with a demon wasn't enough? What gets worse? Wait!" She held out a hand in a 'stop' motion. "Don't answer that. I don't want to borrow trouble."

"Yeah, we have enough of that." I gave a small laugh that wasn't really amused.

"So what's the plan?"

"Wait to see if they get the sword. And try and call Granny's spirit." I shrugged. "It's not perfect but I'm not sure what else to do. You know, outside of give up and let the demon win."

"Come on, now Desi. That's not even an option. And where's your famous 'screw you' optimism?"

"It's taking a beating," I confessed. "I'm afraid."

"We have to win," Deirdre said. "It's that simple. We have to."

I leaned against the counter. "I know. I know. But what—"

"No. Don't even go there. What's going on, Desi?" She put her hand on my arm.

I ran my hand through my hair. "It's Hell. I mean, the literal Hell. I don't want to go back," I whispered. "If Beeval hadn't helped me, I don't know how I would have gotten away. And that scares the shit out of me."

"Stop. Right now. That's how Ashlar wins. That's part of what demons do—suck the life and hope out of things. Don't let him any further, Desi. You can stop this."

"What if we can't?"

"We will. We have to." Deirdre enveloped me in a hug.

I had to be strong for the Deanas. They were scared, even though they were all putting on a brave front and really taking on a lot. But right now, being able to share with my sister, and have her tell me things were going to be okay—I felt better than I had since Ashlar showed up on our street.

I might have even shed a few tears, which were gone by the

time Deirdre let go of me. "You're right," I said, rubbing my face. "We have to win. Thanks," I added.

"No problem."

"What are you making?"

"Killing spells," she said grimly. "I am not happy, but I don't think it's fair to leave the Deanas unprotected."

"How many are you making?" I asked. She had to have a pile of at least twenty.

"As many as I can. I'll charge them when I run out of the ingredients."

I nodded. "I don't know that they'll kill him, though. Even though it's a good thought."

"Yeah, but they might slow him down, and give them some extra time."

To run, to hide ... it was a good idea. "Okay. Have you heard from Dee or Deana?"

Deirdre shook her head. "No."

"That's not good, is it?"

She shook her head again.

"All right, I'll go see if I can track them down. They have a flight back tonight." I gave her shoulder a pat and pulled out my phone.

I texted Deana. *'Hey, how goes it?'*

I watched the message chat and then the dots showed up that someone was typing.

'We got it. But PITA. Figuring out shipping. Flight back tonight. Call in a bit.'

I showed it to Deirdre.

"Call Daniella. I know she's worried too."

"After I tell DeAnna. She nearly bit my head off on the way back from Zane's."

"She's worried, and this is a hell of a way to find out you could be magic, or something."

"True. Call me if you need help. I'm off to spread the good

news. I'll need some help getting all the herbs together for the summoning," I added.

"Sure, I'm here for you. Slaving away in the basement dungeon, the little family troll," Deirdre called as I walked back upstairs.

"Good!" I shouted. "We need people to know their place!"

I heard her laugh, and I called Daniella. "Hey," I said, when she picked up, before she went into the standard greeting.

"What's up?"

"They got it. Deana said it was done, but not easy. They're coming home tonight."

"Thank the goddess," she breathed. "What else?"

"We were texting. Nothing, but she's calling later. How's it going?"

"I'm getting the things together I think might be helpful, and warding the hell out of the shop. In case we need to run."

"Gotcha. Smart thinking."

"We need a hidey hole," she said.

"Is it ready?"

"Yep. All set."

"Excellent." I hung up, and felt a teeny bit better. We had a hidey hole in the back of the shop. At one point, our building had been a bank. There was a vault built into the back of the building, down in the basement, in the rock. We'd had it prepped for ourselves in case of a disaster, and so far, had never had to use it. It had gradually become storage.

I hoped we wouldn't need it. Although I was amazed we'd gotten as much time as we had. Ashlar wasn't a very organized guy. I would have never let this kind of thing slip through my fingers. First me, and then Beeval? How had he missed it?

Unless he was letting us stew—but I didn't think so. I think Beeval was right in that I wasn't his main focus, and he was busy. Which was kind of hilarious if it wasn't happening to me.

A demon too busy for a spot of torture? What the heck was his business?

I didn't want to know. I realized DeAnna didn't know, and walked through the main level looking for her. When I didn't find her, I ran up the stairs.

She was in the upstairs nook, talking with Doc. I stopped, listening.

She was asking what he remembered about Meema, and her mom. No need to get up in that. I had enough going on. "Knock, knock," I said, making sure to make noise in case DeAnna wanted to keep things private.

She touched her cheek and looked up. "Hi. Sorry. I was talking with Doc about Momma."

"No worries. I wanted to let you know I'd heard from Deana."

Her expression brightened instantly. "You did? Are they all right?"

"Yes, and they got the sword. She plans on being on the flight home tonight."

"Oh, thank God," DeAnna said. "So that's the plan?"

"I think we still need to talk to Granny."

DeAnna visibly sighed. "I was hoping you wouldn't say that. I'm very nervous about this."

"What was it you said, Doc?" I faced him. "That you weren't looking forward to hearing someone's truth because it was probably going to make you look bad?" He'd made a comment in that vein when we'd found the diaries. "I feel the same way about this. That whatever we find, it's going to be a complete mess, and I'm going to want to kill Granny."

"She is the font of a great deal of the distress we're dealing with now," Doc said, but his words didn't have the ring of condemnation they'd had even a day earlier.

Which made me glad. I didn't want to be pissed at Granny,

or Meema, whom I suspected would come in for some share in what had happened.

"Do you want to wait for everyone to get back before trying to find Granny?" DeAnna said.

"No. They have a car, they'll get themselves home. I think we do this today, tonight. I don't want to wait. This may take a while with Granny's spirit. I also think you need to make yourself scarce," I added to Doc.

He sighed. "You're probably right, although I must say I have a curiosity to see Desi again."

"Well lurk out of sight if you must, okay?"

"Fair enough, Desdemona."

"When do you want to do this?"

"As soon as Deirdre and Daniella finish. I'm going down to the stillroom and get the stuff I need. Call me if you need me." I gave both of them a brief smile and left.

DeAnna deserved the right to get to know Doc on her own terms. And to have a little peace before the shit hit the fan. Because if we couldn't find Granny, I was going to call up Deana, my long-lost sister.

CHAPTER FIFTEEN

I spent the next two hours in quiet working beside Deirdre. Daniella came home, having shut down things at the shop for the day. People had respected the sign she'd put up—that we'd open in two more days.

I had Zane's book of spirit recall procedures, although it wasn't written that technically. And we prepared the mixtures we'd need to light and burn, as well as getting candles made with grave dirt.

Yes, there was such a thing. We sold them online, along with our tea and herbs. One of the ways it was used was to call forth the spirit of loved one. It didn't mention calling those who might have passed into the light a long time ago. That was where things got fuzzy.

"Well, we have everything," I said.

My phone buzzed. It was Deana again. *'About to board. We'll see you soon, goodies in hand.'*

'Fantastic. Granny might be here to say hi,' I texted back.

'Whoa. Okay. Duly noted.'

So at least that was on track. Back to business. "You all ready?"

My sisters nodded.

"We should get DeAnna in here, so all four of us are represented," Deirdre said.

"I'll get her." Daniella sprinted up the stairs.

Deirdre was reading through the spells we'd need to do. "We're going to have to say these together. And light the grave candle, and then sprinkle more dirt on the herbs, and then light them on fire, too."

"Lots of fire here."

"I wonder if it's meant to be cleansing," Deirdre mused. "It's not very logical."

"That's because we're supposed to let the dead rest," I said. "If they want to hang around, that's one thing. That's their choice. But we're supposed to let the dead be."

"Yeah, I know. Unbunch your panties."

Deirdre was always the one who asked why, and liked to figure that aspect out. "They're not in a bunch. I just want this to work, and to get the answers we need from Granny."

Daniella and DeAnna came back in. DeAnna looked unsettled. I totally understood.

"We're ready?" Daniella asked.

"Yes," I said. "DeAnna, can you read Latin? Or at least read this?" I turned the book to her and showed her.

She began to read.

"Supra et infra spiritibus
nostrae vocationis audiat
Ad eos qui nos ad pallii
Salvos nos fac Domime O spirituum,
Nos atque piae.
Deferrent nostrae
Sine ulla peccatum."

DeAnna stumbled over the unfamiliar words. "I'm not doing it now, am I?" She looked alarmed.

"No, we have to have all the things in place. Magic doesn't

usually happen accidentally. It's why there are usually two or more steps, or you'd have beginning practitioners blowing themselves up all the time," Deirdre said, smiling. "You're good. Go over it a few more times. We're going to say together, so it's not like we're leaving you hanging on your own."

DeAnna mouthed the words, and after watching her, I helped Daniella get all the herbs ready. The grave dirt was in a separate bowl and would be added right before we lit the whole mess on fire.

I didn't like grave dirt. It smelled. I know it was probably a lot of my imagination, but it always smelled to me. At least down here, the smells of everything else muted it.

Finally, DeAnna looked up. "I think that is as good as it's going to get. I'm nervous, so I can't guarantee I'll say it all correctly."

"It'll be fine." Daniella waved her hand. "Okay, ladies, let's do this." She pulled things from the counter, and started placing them on our compass rose on the floor.

"I didn't even notice that," DeAnna said.

"It's better to have a circle to protect you when you're dealing with spirits. We don't do it often, but a circle with the Rose of the Winds—that's an old name for the compass rose—and calling on the spirits of the winds will help you if something you bring through has less than nice intentions," Daniella said.

On the north, she placed the Earth bundle, which was a large quartz crystal. On east, she set down the Air object, an incense holder burning a sage joss stick.

For south, which represented Fire, a plain white candle, clear and clean. Daniella lit it, and the flame flared up strong and bright yellow. And for the west, water in an abalone shell. It made a circle about eight feet in diameter, which was large enough for all of us to stand in, with everyone at a compass direction. We'd need to be closer, so that we could all read from the book.

But here, Deirdre surprised me. She handed out sheets of paper. "One for everyone. That way, we're closer to the Rose points."

"Good call, sister."

"Only took you a hundred years to appreciate me, but I'll take it."

I wondered when she'd done it, and then figured it didn't matter. She'd done it. It would make this all easier. You know, as easy as it could be.

"We ready?" I asked. Now that Meema was gone, leading the work would fall to me, and I wasn't yet comfortable in the role. I'd always been the one who charged ahead, and Meema was there to make sure I didn't fall.

Now I not only had to keep myself from falling, but everyone else. Please, goddess, let this work, I prayed. I looked at my paper, and at my sisters—all four of them, which made me smile—and nodded.

Deirdre brought over the grave candle and lit it. Daniella lit the bowl with the herbs and the grave dirt. A sickly smell drifted up—I really hated the smell of the grave dirt. The herbs only slightly hid it when things were on fire.

I nodded again. "This is for real, now." We all read, speaking slowly.

"Supra et infra spiritibus
nostrae vocationis audiat
Ad eos qui nos ad pallii
Salvos nos fac Domime O spirituum,
Nos atque piae.
Deferrent nostrae
Sine ulla peccatum."

Chanting together, we completed the incantation three times.

I held up a hand. The room had darkened, and the candles were flickering wildly. The temperature dropped and there was a swirling of dust in the middle of the circle.

"We call the spirit of Desdemona Delilah Nightingale, beloved mother of Desdemona, and grandmother to Desdemona, Deirdre, Daniella and Deana. Desdemona Nightingale, we call you!"

There was silence, and the dirt began to swirl more, rising up in the air. Up, and up it rose, gathering more dirt from who knew where. The thought that it was from our stillroom made me a little itchy.

The dirt darkened, and began to take shape. A head, then hair on the head in the form of a bun, and then a skirt. The dirt swirled as the spirit took on more of the characteristics of the human she'd been.

I still didn't know whether it was Granny. The dirt was swirling too fast; too—

"Why have you called me, girls?"

It was Granny.

"Mary, mother of God," DeAnna breathed.

"No, Desdemona, mother of Little Desi," Granny said.

Her voice didn't have her usual snap, and that made me really, really nervous.

"Why did you call me, girls?"

She knew. Holy shit, she knew. "Because we're in a bit of a pile of crap, Granny, and I think it's your crap."

The ghost sighed. "You would be Desdemona, wouldn't you?"

At my look, she waved a hand at me. "Don't get all shirty with me, missy! The last time I saw you, you were ten years old."

"Yeah, when you died on us," Deirdre cut in.

Granny whirled around. "You are?"

"Deirdre." She crossed her arms.

"You have grown into the spitfire I saw when you were little." Granny's face took on an expression of softness.

"And? What did you do? We are in a world of shit, and it all keeps pointing to you!" Deirdre shouted.

Granny sighed again. "I'm going to guess I'm here for a while? Where's Meema? And who are you?" She looked to DeAnna.

"That is DeAnna, daughter of Deana." I kept my voice neutral.

Granny's face shifted to ... guilty. "Where is Deana?"

"She's gone. She's been gone for some time," DeAnna said. "And she never stopped being angry about something that happened here. Was it something with you?"

Granny frowned. "I just said I haven't seen the girls since they were ten." Her eyes, such as they were, shifted around.

"Granny, what aren't you telling us?" She was hiding something.

"Where should I start?" she asked finally.

"At the beginning," Daniella said. "Because there's a lot your diaries don't cover. Not that we've read all of them, just the parts about Ashlar and you welshing on your agreement!"

"You're taking his side in this?" Granny held a hand to her chest. "Really? If you've met him, you know that he isn't a good being. No demons are. But he's a particularly bad one."

"And so that was the one you made a deal with?" I demanded. "You need to start explaining."

"Where's Meema?" Granny asked again.

"She's in Hell," I said flatly. "Where Ashlar took her, and me, less than a week ago. He tossed her soul into the River of Souls. He tied me up, meaning to torture me while my body decayed in Hell. Only by the grace of a demon did I get away, and I have no idea how to find or rescue Meema's soul. All we know is that Ashlar says you didn't honor your agreement, and now we're on clean-up detail."

"Don't forget the whole trying to stay alive detail," Deirdre put in. "Because the demon is pissed, and said that since you'd already died, the contract would never be fulfilled, so the Nightingale women would have to pay the price forever!" Her hands were on her hips as she glared at Granny.

I saw something out of the corner of my eye, and I slid my gaze over. Granny might be dead, but she was sharp as ever, and I didn't want to distract her.

Doc was hovering half in, half out of the wall. I widened my eyes and shook my head. Granny didn't need to see him right now. I wasn't sure how she'd receive him, since she'd gone out of her head over this guy. He frowned at me.

I glared back.

He sank back into the wall. Thank the Goddess. We had enough drama to be going on with right now.

"Well, you'd better get chairs, girls. I'll tell you about the demon."

Daniella stepped out of the circle, and got a chair for everyone, placing them inside the circle.

As we sat, Granny watched all of us, turning from first one to the other. "It's very good to see you girls. I'm sorry that Deana's gone." An expression I couldn't read crossed her face. "But I'm glad to meet her daughter. Was she happy?" she asked DeAnna.

"Yes and no," DeAnna said. "She was not happy to have left her home, but she was also really glad to be out of Deadwood.

Granny sighed. There was a lot of that going around and it made me nervous as hell.

"Okay, Granny, you've stalled long enough. Spill. Why did you make a deal with a demon? And even more so, why with Ashlar? He's a complete asshole," I said.

"Because he was the demon who showed up when I called him," Granny said calmly, like that explained anything.

"Just because he dangled immortality in front of you, or

Doc, didn't mean you had to say yes!" I struggled to keep my voice down. "Look at me!" I pulled up my sleeve. "This is part of what it cost me to get out of Hell! I had to crawl out, my skin on fire! Now you tell us why you did it! Make me understand why this was necessary!"

"I did it for you girls." Granny's voice was soft, her eyes riveted on the black marks that went up my arm. "How did you get out of Hell?"

"I crawled out. On my hands and knees, not sure if I was going to make it. I'm not the same. I have nightmares of the River of Souls. I can hear Meema!" Damn it, I needed to calm down. This wasn't going the way I thought it would.

"How long did the Cannadys last?"

"Years," Daniella said. "They made it years. Finally, the daughter broke and laughed in Ashlar's face."

"In all that time, he never came back to Deadwood to check. He's not very smart, for a demon." Granny looked over our heads, seeing something we couldn't.

Which was the damn problem.

"Well, he was smart enough to kill Meema, and nearly kill me. No thanks to you. Granny, how could you do this to us? You had to know that we'd figure it out, and then have to deal with this!" I exclaimed.

"I did not know. I'd already determined that Ashlar wasn't the brightest demon of the bunch."

"What, you know a lot?" Deirdre asked, rolling her eyes.

"Don't take that tone with me, young lady. I know a sight more than you do."

"No, shit," Deirdre shot back. "It would've been great had you shared before you know, you died on us."

"I am trying to share now," Granny said with exaggerated patience. "May I continue?" After a moment of silence, she went on. "I figured that he'd never find out. He was, at the time, vain and proud, and that sort of man, be he human or demon, tends to get in his own way. So I figured Mrs. Cannady and Tandy, her daughter, would be able to fool him."

"You condemned them to that?"

"I made a bargain with them. They knew I was a yarb woman, a healer, and came to me anyway. They knew they would die. At the time, consumption was fatal. I told them if they did me a service, I'd make sure the other four children were taken care of. You don't understand what it was like for children with no adults to care for them. They felt they got a good bargain. And I kept it. Every one of those children found a good home. They were still close to their siblings, and had a good chance. Better than they had with Mrs. Cannady. No one would do anything for a consumptive woman." Granny didn't sound the least bit repentant.

"I've been in Hell, Granny. It was horrible."

"Yes, I am sure it was. But there are many kinds of Hell, Desdemona. Leaving your children behind is another."

"You'd know," snapped Deirdre. "I love Doc, but really, Granny, you did all this for a man?"

Granny stared at Deirdre, and then burst out laughing. "You think I did all this for John Henry? Oh, my Lord," and she doubled over laughing.

I saw Doc's head emerge from the wall out of the corner of my eye. I pretended not to notice him. He felt horrible that Granny had gone mad over him. Apparently that wasn't the case, so I figured he had a right to hear this.

"Oh, my," Granny said. "I adored that man, I admit. And he gave me the most wonderful gift ever, your mother, girls. Well, your grandmother," she added to DeAnna. "I did indeed want to settle down with him, and by the time he was ready to leave Deadwood, I could have helped him. I do believe I could have cured him. But he left, and took up with Big Nose Kate, so that, as they say, was that." She laughed again. "It's because of him we have this house—he could do wonders with a hand of cards, even an awful hand. But that—well, that is not why I bargained with Ashlar."

"Then why in the name of blazes did you keep me here?" Doc charged through then, coming to a stop outside our Rose of the Winds circle. "I wanted to pass on. You knew that, and you kept me here."

Granny had turned when Doc spoke, and her eyes widened as she listened to him. She didn't answer, her hand covering her mouth.

"Answer me, woman! Damn it! I've been stuck here for over one hundred years! No right to the rest that all beings should have! I love these girls, but it has not been easy for any of us!"

"You're still here," she whispered. "Oh, my. John Henry, you look as good as you ever did."

"That is not important, Desdemona. Why did you keep me here? Why did you bring me in the first place? And most importantly, why in God's name did you truck with a demon? And leave it to your granddaughters, our granddaughters, to deal with? Do you know that I watched our daughter disappear before my eyes?"

I didn't think ghosts could cry, but Granny sure looked close.

Whatever she was going to say was interrupted by the slam of a door and footsteps above our heads.

"This has got to be the worst séance ever," Daniella muttered. "We suck at this."

"No we don't," I whispered back. "We got our girl. But we have too many ghosts, and way too much drama."

She covered her mouth, trying not to laugh. I had to do the same. It was either that or scream and cry, and the latter wouldn't do a damn thing for any aspect of this situation.

"Hey! We're home! And we got it! Where is everyone?" Deana's voice rang out. "Gran? Desdemona?"

"Let's just throw a party," Deirdre muttered. "We're down here!" she yelled.

Footsteps thundered down the stairs and Deana came in, waving a small silver and gold sword. It was a cross between a fancy hunting knife and a real sword. It gleamed even in the dim light of the stillroom.

"You got it," I whispered. I felt tears spring to the back of my eyes. Till this moment, I hadn't been sure they'd get it, that it was real. "Are you sure this is the right thing?"

"Touch it," Zane said, coming from behind Deana and Dee, who were hugging DeAnna.

He took it from Deana, and handed it to me. I touched it, and the electricity bolted through me.

"That's angel magic," he said, and there was a fire in his eyes. Then he took in the scene. "Holy shit."

"Exactly. Everyone, this is the much-vaunted Granny, who was just telling us the real deal."

You could have heard a pin drop in the stillroom.

Everyone turned to Granny.

CHAPTER SIXTEEN

"Well, I'm not sure what all the fuss is about. Yes, I made a deal with Ashlar. I fulfilled the bargain, two souls for the gifts he gave me."

"What did he give you?"

"Immortality for me and my descendants, as long as we wanted it."

"If we stayed in Deadwood," Daniella cut in.

"He did tack that on without telling me about it first," Granny admitted. "He also gave you to me," she added in the direction of Doc. "I didn't tell him I wanted you. I told him I was so sad because I wanted to save you, and if I could do that, you might have stayed. You left, and he laughed at me. He knew I was expecting—he was the one who told me, sadly. He told me if I agreed to our bargain, I could have everything I wanted."

"Well, he wasn't entirely honest with you, then," I said. "But you said you wanted love—"

"No, he was not honest," Granny cut me off. "And I did want love. I got it, in your mother, and you girls," she looked at us fondly. "But I was proud. And that was my sin, girls. I thought I could outwit a demon. After all, he wasn't the brightest, or the most cunning—but he is a demon."

"Okay, whatever. How do we beat him?" Deirdre asked. "Tell us, keeper of all the answers."

I continued where Deirdre left off. "Because he's coming back. The clock is ticking. I'm astounded we haven't heard from him yet. And worse, Granny, he'll screw up all of Deadwood in the process. We got lucky when we were able to ward it before. There's only three of us now that Meema is gone." I couldn't stop myself from butting in. Just in case she was tempted to wander too far down memory lane.

She looked around. "I see six of you."

"These are Deana's girls. They weren't raised in magic like we were."

"Deana left, didn't she?" Granny seemed sad, but not surprised.

"Yes, she did. Why was that, I wonder?"

"I came back. I came back to tell you all what had happened. I wanted to warn you, and try to make things right. There was much I had to tell you." She stopped. I'd never seen a ghost look so uncomfortable. When no one said anything, she continued, although I could tell she would have rather have changed the subject, or lopped off her head, or anything other than this. "I wanted to make sure John Henry was free. My death should have set him on his way to the light—"

"It didn't," Doc said. He'd taken up leaning against the wall of the stillroom, against one of our cabinets, to be exact.

"I am sorry, John Henry. Truly, I am. I thought my death would set you free."

"It did not. Nor could I leave your quarters."

"That was me," she confessed. "I didn't want you surprising the girls, or guests. How did you get out?"

"Little Desi was able to extend the spell to the house," Doc said without any inflection.

I noted that when he was really angry, his voice remained calm, but his accent got stronger.

"She always was a smart girl," Granny said. "I'm so sorry that Ashlar got her."

"We read in your diaries that you were trying to spare her," Daniella said.

"Oh, I was. From the demon, and from—" She stopped.

"Yes?" I prompted.

"It doesn't matter. I wanted and intended a lot of things," Granny said briskly. "And I failed. So let us concentrate on the matter at hand. What do you need from me?"

"Help defeating Ashlar. He won't stop."

"We have the angel sword," said Dee, who'd been quiet until now.

"It's extraordinary how all three of you look so much like Deana," Granny said wistfully. "I am so sorry she's not with us anymore."

"What do you know about it?" I asked. This trip down memory lane wasn't entirely honest. I could feel it.

"What do you mean?" Granny looked coy, innocent.

Like she was lying by omission.

"I mean, what do you know about Deana leaving?"

"She was pissed," Daniella said. Her face had the same expression as Granny's.

I glanced back and forth between them. It was extraordinary, but since we hadn't seen Granny since we were girls, it made sense that we wouldn't know. I knew Daniella well enough to know that her calm expression held back a potential anger, and it made me wonder, again, what Granny was hiding.

Granny sighed. "She was angry. I came back, as I said, and I tried to tell her— Well, it doesn't matter—"

"I think it does," Deirdre interrupted.

"No, it really doesn't. But I was trying to see if I could get in contact, and talk with Desi, and I met Deana instead. She was upset with me—"

"But why?" I asked. Something wasn't adding up.

"It doesn't matter now. It seemed important at the time, but it wasn't."

"How can that be?" Doc asked. "It was important enough for you to come back, that means it was important."

Granny gave Doc a look that could have cut him off at the knees had either of them been living. "Fine. I wanted to talk to Desi—your mother." She looked at me. "About some of my family."

"Yeah, that would be nice information to have," Daniella said, her expression still neutral.

"Well, I would agree," Granny sighed. "But that is neither here nor there. What is it I can help you girls with right now?"

"What do we need to know about the demon? What haven't you shared?" I asked. I was done with this dancing around the subject. "And why the hell didn't you tell us? Is that what you told Deana?" I asked, remembering how DeAnna and I had talked about Deana leaving abruptly. "Is that what pissed her off? Did you tell her about Ashlar?"

Granny nodded, although a look of relief crossed her face, and I made a note of it.

"What was her reaction?"

"Well, she was angry. She wanted to know why I'd doomed your mother. And how dare I do that to her? She called me selfish, and short-sighted."

"She was right," Deirdre said.

Granny inhaled. I could see it because her nostrils flared slightly, and the atmosphere in the room got warm. She was getting pissed at all the asides. Tough shit. It was time she dealt with what she'd done, what she'd left others to clean up.

"Well, hindsight is a wonderful thing to have. I did what I needed to do," Granny said, lips tight. "It might not have been the best thing, with that lovely hindsight, but it was the best I could do at the time."

"Why did you think we needed to be immortal?" I asked, thinking about some of the things Granny had said about the deal she'd made with Ashlar.

"Because if you're going to be a witch—and since it was part of my family, I figured any descendants of mine would be—you might come up against less than nice creatures. I wanted you all, even before I knew there was a 'you all', to be safe."

"It's probably a good thing we like Deadwood," Daniella said.

"I know it's not ideal. But—" Granny began.

"No buts," I said. "We need to figure out what else could happen. Is there anything else you can tell us, Granny? Anything else about Ashlar we need to know?"

She shook her head, the pale edges of her form blurring as she moved. "He's not as smart as he thinks he is, and he's motivated by pride above all else. He loves to gloat, so if he thinks he's won something, that's better for you. His anger also drives him." She shrugged. "I didn't have that many interactions with him. Had he not been a very poor winner, I would have seen him only twice."

"Okay. That's good to know." I nodded. "Anyone else have questions for Granny?"

"I'd like to speak with you for a bit," Doc said, drifting closer.

Granny watched him, her face unreadable. "Very well."

"After you, my dear." Doc stepped aside and gave her a half-bow, a mocking smile on his face.

He and Granny faded into the wall.

"Hey! We weren't done, were we?" Deana looked around.

"Get a room! And not one of ours!" Deirdre yelled loudly.

"I'm not sure that gave us much," Dee said.

"Oh my God, tell us about Gareth." Daniella turned to Dee

and Deana. "I was worried you weren't going to be able to pry it out of him."

"He didn't know what it was. He knew it was magical, but he didn't know how much," Zane said, a slight smile curving up the corner of his lips.

Why did I always feel so much better when he was around? It bothered me. I couldn't think about anyone, much less him. And certainly not right now. For goddess' sake.

"He was a loathsome little creep," Deana said.

Unexpectedly, Dee laughed. "He took a shine to Deana. She had to sit next to him, and coax him to humor her weird old mom."

"You owe me." Deana rubbed her arms, looking disgusted. "Seriously. Big time. He say way too close."

"I know. But if we can get rid of the demon, and make it easier for us to live in peace, is that enough?"

"No. There needs to be more," Deana said, still grumpy. "That guy was the grossest person I've met in ages."

"Was he dirty or something?" Daniella asked.

"No, he was actually meticulous, and neat, considering his affinity for grave dirt."

"The thing he liked more than Deana," Zane said.

Deana made a face, and all of us laughed.

"Well, all right, then. We're ready for this demon?" DeAnna asked.

"We didn't need to use any of your spells," Dee said. "I was ready, but nothing happened that we felt necessitated them."

"I don't know that those will work on him," Deirdre said. "But they might slow him down. Hang onto them."

"So now we just wait? Can't we call him out, or something?" Deana asked.

Silence greeted her question.

CHAPTER SEVENTEEN

"Are you insane? We want to stay away from the demon!" DeAnna was horrified. "Don't we?"

"Well, yes," I said slowly. Deana's idea wasn't the worst ever.

"It would get it all over," Deirdre said.

"And then we'd have some kind of resolution, either way," Daniella added.

"This is why Mom left," DeAnna said. "I spent some time thinking about what you asked, for me to remember the things she did say..." This was directed at me. "And what she always said was that she didn't want to spend her entire life—even though she didn't tell us about living forever—running headlong into danger at all times."

I met my sisters' gaze. "It's a fair criticism."

"But she didn't used to be that way," Daniella said. "She loved it as much as we did. She was the fastest one with zombies out of all of us." She glanced around, grinning. "She could chop off a head in a few seconds."

"She never told us any of that, that's for damn sure," Deana said.

"Well, she probably didn't want any of us running off to join the crazy aunts in Deadwood," Dee said easily.

"We're not—" Deirdre began, and then she looked at Daniella and me.

We all burst into laughter.

"Yes, we are," I said, trying to calm myself. "We totally are." Which made all three of us, as well as the Deanas and Zane, laugh.

This, more than anything else, made me hopeful. We were here, with family, and the wounds of the past seemed like they had a chance of healing. With a few bumps in the road. This was the kind of strength, the kind of bond, that would come together to bring down a demon.

I hoped. But I had to hope. I didn't want to die, and I didn't want me, my sisters, or the Deanas harassed to literal death.

"So we're going to pick a fight?" Deirdre said.

"I think we should. Deana is right. We don't want to sit around here, twiddling our thumbs and picking fights with each other—" I said.

"We tend to fight," Daniella interrupted.

"When we could be expending our energy on kicking his ass," I finished.

"Are we sure we're going to kick it?" DeAnna asked. Her arms were crossed, and she was frowning.

"No." Deirdre turned to her. "We're never sure we're going to kick anyone's ass. We're never sure we're going to win. But we go in and do our best, because we owe that to the people here. We agreed to protect them. And now, we're protecting ourselves —us, and the three of you. Probably you, too," she added, including Zane in her statement. "You help us, and you'll be considered aligned with us."

"I'm good with that," he said. "I know the risks."

Something in the way he said that caught my—attention?

Danger radar? But before I could ask him, Deirdre continued, focusing her attention on the Deanas.

"You don't have to fight. You can sit this one out. I won't think any less of you. I don't really want to take on the greasy asshole, and I've been doing this my entire life. You haven't. It's up to you. We don't force anyone to do anything they don't want to. But this is going to happen, and we do have to deal with it. Like it or not, you're a Nightingale, and you get your share of the shit like everyone else."

Well, that went south fast. Everyone else seemed to think so as well, because no one replied.

"I appreciate your honesty," DeAnna said to Deirdre. "I don't much like it, but I appreciate it. I need to think about it. My life may seem short compared to yours, but I'm afraid, and I'm not ashamed to admit it."

"Mom," Dee said, just as Deana said, "Gran!"

DeAnna held up a hand. "It's my right, because we're talking about my life, about all your lives," she said to her daughter and granddaughter.

"Exactly, Gran," Deana said. "Which is why you need to get off your ass and take a stand. You've always been cautious, probably because Grammy was. But this isn't that time. If you're not willing to do it for our aunts, which is kind of bullshit in my opinion, but whatever, then you need to do it for yourself. At the very least. I'm kind of ashamed of your thought process here. I was raised better than this."

"Yes, you were!" DeAnna might be cautious, but she wasn't taking this lying down.

I kept my mouth shut. This wasn't my fight.

"There's fighting for something right, and suicide! This is suicide! How are we, a bunch of human women, going to defeat a demon? I can't even think about it without peeing my pants a little!"

"TMI, Mom," Dee said.

"He is scary, but when you see him, the first thing you think is that he's just disgusting," Daniella said.

"Well, not me," I said. "He scares the piss out of me, too. I don't want to go back," I let everyone see, hopefully, how scared I was. "I've never been scared of much but Hell scares the shit out of me."

DeAnna sighed. "I need to think about it. I'm not happy about this, and I'm struggling because Mom was so firm on not wanting to be involved with anything happening here. I can't help but think she was right." She held up a hand as Deana opened her mouth, probably to protest. "I know your thoughts, and I hear them. But I need to think. Now if you will excuse me, I'm going up to the room." She got up and walked up the stairs.

We could hear her in the kitchen and then heading up to the bedrooms.

"I'm with you," Dee said.

"Me too," Deana added.

"Your mom is entitled to however she feels," Daniella said, her tone and expression calm. "I respect it. This isn't the life for everyone. It's all we've known." She shrugged. "So it's not that big of a deal to us. I mean, it is, but this comes along with being a witch, and protecting Deadwood. You run into some shit."

"Why don't we all go get something to eat, and then get some sleep?" Zane stepped into the conversation with a much-needed detour.

He'd been so quiet I'd almost forgotten he was there.

"If Ashlar shows up, can you ward the houses for an alarm?" Zane continued. "Something to give us a few moments?"

I looked at Daniella. She nodded.

"We can," Deirdre said. "It will be stronger if you two help us. You're Nightingales."

"Okay," Dee said. "Just tell us what we need to do."

"Let's go eat. I also need to check on Beeval. I haven't seen him much today."

With that, we trooped up the stairs to the kitchen. Without words, Deirdre, Daniella and I started to assemble dinner. Steak, potatoes, and salad. We kept a lot of it on hand, since it was a favorite and easy to prepare.

As soon as the potatoes started to boil, Beeval wandered in.

"Where have you been all day?" I asked.

He was missing his Evil hat.

"Seeking," he said.

"What for?" I asked. I noted that no one else seemed to be as comfortable as I was. That made sense. I couldn't be anything other than comfortable with the guy who'd saved me.

"Ashlar," he said.

"What? He's here?" I nearly dropped the knife I was holding.

The entire kitchen full of people had gone still, all focused on the little demon.

Beeval shook his head. "No. Fuzzy things that way"—He pointed toward Mrs. Kittrick's—"say smells bad, but the bad smeller not come back. They saw him," he added. "When he come here. They remember, hide but still scared."

"You're talking to the cats?" I asked. Why was everyone else talking to the cats? I didn't know if I was jealous, or jealous that I hadn't thought of it first.

Beeval nodded. "I go say hello. Good to know what else lives here." He looked up at me, and gave a wide-toothed approximation of a grin.

"Meeting the neighbors is always a good idea," Zane said with a straight face.

"Can you cast magic? Or spells?" Deirdre asked Beeval.

"My magic little. Small. But some," he answered her.

I wondered what counted for small in demon terms.

"Like what? What do you do?" Daniella leaned down, peering at him.

"Blast," Beeval said, flinging his hands out in front of him. "Stop moving. Bind," he glanced up at me again, and his eyes were sad. "I bind you. So I let you go."

I knelt down, reaching out for him instinctively. "I know you did. I'm alive because of you." He stepped closer to me, leaning against my shoulder.

One of his long arms came up to pat me clumsily on the shoulder.

"I never thought I'd see the day when we were all sniffly over a demon," Deirdre said.

I shot her a glare. Really? This was not the time.

"But I'm glad I'm seeing it," she finished. "Thank you, Beeval. We're all glad you're here."

Beeval gazed around at everyone in the kitchen. They were all nodding. He smiled. "Beeval help. I help," he repeated.

"Against Ashlar?" Daniella asked.

He nodded. "Yes. I help. If he gets me, I am dead." The finality, the certainty in his voice left no room for doubt.

"Well, it seems that we're all in the same boat," Deana said. "How old are you, Beeval?"

Beeval shrugged. "Many years."

"You hungry?" I asked him.

"Bacon?" he asked hopefully.

"Always," Deirdre said. She went to the fridge and pulled out a package. We'd bought a lot of bacon this week to keep up with Beeval.

At least if he was friends with Evil and the cats next door, I didn't have to worry about him eating them.

Dinner was a quiet affair. DeAnna didn't come back downstairs, and Dee made her a plate without any comment. Deana and Dee cleaned up, and then everyone went to their rooms. I had barely made it into my room when there was a knock.

"Come in."

Deirdre and Daniella filed in. "We need to call this douchebag, and get this over, one way or another," Deirdre said.

"I agree. So how do we call him? I have to tell you, I haven't been scared in a long time, but he scares the shit out of me. I know it's not rational, but I don't want to lie to you," I said.

"It's understandable. I think, because I've been thinking about this," Daniella said, "that you and Beeval should keep out of sight unless you have to show your faces. There's no sense in letting him know you're here if he doesn't know."

"How can I do that and help you?"

"We need to call him out in the road. Not on our land, but outside of our boundaries. I'll set a ward around the property lines. You and Beeval can be in the house, in the window. That way, you're right there, but you're not immediately visible," Deirdre replied. It was apparent she and Daniella had been not only thinking about this but discussing it.

"That might work," I said slowly.

"It's better than putting you out in the open and exposing you right from the get-go," Daniella said. "I'd prefer you to be the element of surprise." She moved to the door. "Beeval," she called.

He appeared as though he'd been waiting. "Dan?"

"Come in and let's talk." She stood back, giving him room to enter.

"Yes?" Beeval looked at the three of us, waiting. Waiting for orders? Like he'd done his whole life?

Before I could say anything about not bossing him around, Daniella continued. "We want to talk about how to handle Ashlar. We're going to bring him here."

Beeval frowned. "Why?"

"Because we don't want to live in a state of waiting," Deirdre said. "Let's bring him here and get this over with. But we thought you and Desdemona should be inside, hidden from him."

"He not know I gone. He come if he know," Beeval said.

"So let's not tell him you're gone unless we have to," I said. "You and I can be out of sight, but we can watch, and we can help."

"I help," Beeval said.

"Are you willing to kill him?" Deirdre asked. "I hope one of us does it, but you might need to be a part of that."

Beeval didn't hesitate. "I kill. I not going back. Not ever."

"Excellent," Deirdre said, and she smiled. It was the first smile I'd seen on her in ages.

"So here's what we're going to do, Beeval," Daniella said.

We spent another thirty minutes going over the plan.

"We're all good?" Deirdre looked around. When everyone nodded, she exhaled. "Good. I'm already tired of this shit hanging over us."

"We kill," Beeval said. His voice was grim, but he sounded sure.

"Yes, we will," Daniella said.

Beeval nodded, and walked out of the room. "I go make sure Evil safe," he said and closed the door behind him.

"You were right, Desi, to bring him here," Daniella said.

"I usually am," I shot back. "But can we change subjects for a sec?"

They both looked at me.

"Granny didn't tell us the whole truth."

"Not that I disagree, but about what?" Deirdre asked.

"There's something more about why Deana left. Something else she learned from Granny," I said. I didn't know what it was, but I felt it in my bones. I knew there was more.

"I got that, too," Daniella said, nodding.

"We have to get the truth out of her. No more secrets," I sighed. "I'm really tired of them screwing up everything."

"Well, it's really Granny's secret. And Deana's, but I think she took that with her when she left," Deirdre frowned.

"If DeAnna knew, she'd have told us, while yelling at us," Daniella said.

We all grinned. "She is the old lady of the bunch," I said. "But I get it."

"I'm glad they're here. I think they needed to know, and it's better to get this shit out. If she wants to hate us, at least she'll have good reason," Deirdre said.

"Not like we haven't been hated before," I replied.

"We're not going to let him take you, or anyone else," Daniella said, coming to hug me.

All three of us came in for a hug. Losing Meema, and then meeting all Deana's girls—it was like Deana had died all over again. And it was made worse because now Meema wasn't here. We stood together for a while.

"So let's do this tomorrow?" Deirdre asked.

Daniella and I nodded. "Tomorrow. We call him, and we kill him."

Everyone went to bed early. It was though there was a feeling of waiting for the other shoe to drop in the entire house. As I fell asleep, I realized we'd not seen Doc or Granny since they disappeared from the stillroom. I hoped one or both of them would be around after this was over.

We'd lost enough already.

CHAPTER EIGHTEEN

The next morning, Deirdre, Daniella and I were up early, cooking again. It soothed us all. Beeval came in, minus Evil.

"Where is Evil?" I asked. "We haven't seen him in two days."

"He safe, away," Beeval replied. "Ashlar not care about small things."

"Maybe tell the cats," Deirdre muttered.

"Did," Beeval said.

After we ate, and there was no sign of the Deanas, we all went outside, and cast a warding spell. Two, actually. One to protect the town, because they sure as hell didn't need to see or hear what was coming, and one to protect our land. Anyone who came close would just wander away, forgetting why they needed to be here.

Essentially, we were removing our home from the daily Deadwood life.

Daniella also warded the area around Pearl Street. Ashlar would have no choice but to come here. I thought when he was summoned, he wouldn't want to come anywhere else, but

Deirdre was of the belief that he'd wreck as much as he could on his way. It was a valid point.

When we came back in, hot and sweating from our efforts, all three of the Deanas were up.

"Good morning," Dee said. "What's on the agenda today?"

Belatedly, I realized we hadn't brought them up to speed on the plans for the day.

"We just set wards for the house and the town. Once you're ready and we go over the plans, we're going to summon Ashlar."

DeAnna spoke before anyone else. "I am going to say I still don't think this is a good idea. But we"—She nodded at Dee and Deana—"spent time talking last night. I'm sorry that I keep getting mad. Some of it is Mom, and some of it is that I'm really afraid. But I want to be able to live in peace, and I want all of you to have peace as well." She stopped, staring down at her hands, and then she sighed. "So I'm in. I'll help where I can. And I promise to do the best I can."

I reached across the island and took her hand. "That's all we can ask. We're going to protect you." I felt good making that promise, although it scared me.

"And you'll have the spells we prepared," Daniella said. "That will slow down anyone who comes for you."

"Will it stop them?" Dee asked.

"Maybe."

"We also have Beeval," I said. "He is not being all that open, but I think he'll be a bigger asset than we realize."

"Are you sure?" DeAnna asked. "You trust him?"

"I do," I said. "He helped get me out of Hell."

"It could be a trick, to make you think he is your friend." Deana looked at me like she was sorry she had to say it, but she had to say it.

"Maybe, but until he shows me he's not trustworthy, we go with he is."

"Even if it risks us all?" DeAnna asked.

"Yes," Deirdre said. "We have to take that chance."

"I don't see why, but I'll go along with your judgement," Dee said. "However, if he gets us hurt, or killed, I will haunt you, and I will be the biggest pain in your ass you've ever met."

To hear Dee, who was fairly low key, not only cuss but threaten was so funny that all six of us burst into laughter, even DeAnna.

A knock on the door startled us all into silence. I went to answer it and it was Zane. "Am I late for the party?" he asked.

"Nope. It's just about to get started." I smiled at him, liking seeing him. And not liking that I liked seeing him. At some point, I needed to deal with this yo-yo shit seeing him brought on. Now wasn't the time. But I was already tired of it.

"Good. I brought all the incantations we need to call him," he added. "I didn't know if you needed them."

"We do," Daniella said. "Calling demons isn't really something we have ever done."

"Then it's good to be useful," Zane said. "What's the plan?"

"We're going to call him, and we're going to kill him. Has anyone seen Doc or Granny?" I asked, struck by the fact that I hadn't. Not since they'd ghosted out of the stillroom last night.

Everyone, even Zane, shook their heads no.

"You don't think they're..." Deirdre began. "No. They can't, can they?"

"What?" I asked. Then I got it. "Hell, no. Is that even possible? Even if it is, who wants to think about that?"

"Is what possible?" Deana asked. Then she looked from me to Deirdre to Daniella. "Holy crap. You think they're getting it on somehow?" She looked at the three of us again and started to laugh. "I don't know, and I sure as hell do not want to know. That is eye bleach territory right there."

"They do know we're planning to summon Ashlar today. They'll be here," Zane said.

"Have you talked to them?" DeAnna asked.

"No. But Doc was here when Ashlar showed up before. I am sure he has impressed upon your grandmother what that was like. They won't miss it." Zane sounded confident.

Damn it. Why did I have to like having him here so much? This looked like an awkward conversation once we'd kicked Ashlar's ass. I was used to the awkward conversations. I'd had a few... well, I guess you could call them boyfriends, over the years. It was all very casual on my end. The trouble came when the other party wasn't quite as casual.

And we hadn't even been naked or anything, but I found that I cared more about him than any guy I could remember in years.

Damn it.

Well, time enough for all the awkward as ass gyrations later. Keeping alive was the main thing right now.

Zane and Daniella handed out all of the herbal aides that Daniella had made, giving more to the Deanas. I watched, wondering if I could convince Deana to stay for a while. She had the most talent, which was odd as she was the furthest removed from Granny and Meema. Maybe it was because she was more open-minded. DeAnna was given to fits of mistrust, and Dee seemed like she enjoyed it, but it would be too much of a bother. She was the chill bridge in that household, I could tell.

But Deana? There was something there. As though she knew I was thinking of her, she happened to look up and smile. Then she pulled something from behind her back, and handed me the angel sword.

In all my worry about everything else, I'd forgotten this. Which was insane. It was the thing that would save us. I was not used to having more people, and things that would help us in our fights. It was usually just us, any spells we had, and our herbals. That was it.

The sword felt good in my hand.

"You might want to keep that out of sight, initially," Zane said. "While my fellow necromancer didn't know what it was, I'll bet that Ashlar knows exactly what it is."

I didn't speak, only nodded, and tucked it down my pant leg. Good thing I was wearing leggings today. Maybe it would conceal this from Ashlar until it was time to pull it out.

And I could hope, shallowly, that I didn't rip my leggings in the process. Potentially dying in only my underwear was not high on my list.

Watching the people around me, I found that not only did I want to live, and deal with awkward Zane moments, but I wanted to teach all that we knew to *someone*. I'd like it best if it was one of our family, one of our someones. Maybe that could be Deana.

After we'd learned about the deal Granny had struck, I'd wondered, a little bitterly, why Granny had chosen to have kids, and why Meema had done the same. But right now, watching my family get ready to save ourselves, I knew why.

"I love you," I said.

Deirdre and Daniella turned immediately. They clasped my hands. "Love you, too," they said in unison. We all hugged.

Then I stepped away, and looked at the Deanas. "One of the things Meema always insisted on was that we tell each other we loved each other before we went out into anything potentially bad. So now you all get to join in. Clasp hands." I held out my hands.

All six of us, and then Zane, gripped each other's hands in a circle. "Love you all," I said.

"Love you, too," everyone echoed.

I felt a pair of arms hug my leg. "I help," Beeval said.

I let go of Deirdre's hand to lean down and put an arm around him. I wondered if I should be worried that his smell didn't seem quite as bad, and if we were going to be like the houses of cat ladies where they never noticed the litter boxes anymore. "I know," I said.

He leaned his head against me. Then he met my eyes. "Evil safe," he said.

"Good. Thank you. Any advice?" I asked.

"Be ready. He clever." Beeval nodded, and looked out the window. "We fight."

"Yes, we do," Daniella said. "Let's go check on the ward one more time. All the wards, in fact." She was referring to warding the town from us, and then warding around Pearl Street so that hopefully Ashlar couldn't get out and go harass our little town. They'd been set this morning, but it didn't hurt to check.

It always seemed when shit went sideways, other supernatural elements jumped in to cause problems and move their own agenda forward. Strong wards would be a good thing on all kinds of levels.

I stood with my sisters as we cast the spells that held the wards. Nothing was amiss. It was a gorgeous day, and the sun was shining. The sky was a vibrant blue, and there were no clouds.

"No sense dawdling," I said. "Let's call his mangy ass."

If I had to die, at least it would be on my terms, in my home, with my family, on a gorgeous day.

Zane held up his arms, and began to chant.

CHAPTER NINETEEN

"Q*uadrato autem dicamus, Ashlar. Precipimus tibi quod ostendam tibi, et stare ante nos.*" Zane spoke slowly, and as he finished the incantation, he paused, then repeated it in the same slow, measured tones. He scattered herbs as he did so, something he must have made because none of us had made it for him.

After listening to him repeat the words several times, we joined him, all six of us. There was a bit of stumbling over the Latin from the Deanas, but I thought they did well.

The ground began to rumble.

"Oh, shit," Deirdre breathed.

"Keep going," I hissed.

The rumbling increased, and a crack burst in the middle of the small road in front of our house. Shit. We'd have to get that fixed before winter.

Red light burst from it, then a plume of dark, dank, evil-smelling vapor.

"Brimstone," Daniella said, wrinkling her nose. "Desi, get inside."

"God, that stinks," Dee said.

"Wait till you see Tall, Dark, and Gross," I muttered. My stomach fluttered, and I felt the nerves rising up in my throat, threatening to upend breakfast. No. I would not puke in front of the demon or anyone else. "Oh, shit! Wait! Take this." I pulled the sword from my pants, not ripping them, which was a plus for me. "Put it down the back of your shirt," I said to Deirdre as I moved inside and went to stand inside the bay window with Beeval.

She tucked it under her shirt, and Daniella moved close to her, with Deana on the other side of Deirdre. It was good to have more than just us.

The crack widened, and I saw Ashlar's horned head begin to emerge.

"What is this, a Vegas show?" Dee asked.

I covered my mouth to keep from laughing.

"Apparently, he wants to make an entrance," DeAnna said.

I wondered where this sass had come from— but I was glad to see it.

Ashlar rose all the way from the crack, and there was a gasp from at least two of the Deanas. I couldn't look to see which of them it was. I had to keep my eyes on him.

When he had fully emerged from the crack—from Hell, I guess—he looked around, getting his bearings. When he saw everyone on the front lawn, he frowned.

"Why have you called me? You shall not have your sister back. She is lost to you." He crossed his arms.

"We haven't called you here for that," Deirdre said. She and Daniella stood shoulder to shoulder, and something in my heart cried to see them standing there, so bravely. I prayed to the goddesses that nothing would happen to my sisters. Or my nieces. Or Zane.

Beeval and I were already on our second lives.

The little demon peered over the window sill. "He not know we gone," he said, his ears flopping as he watched the goings-on in front of us. "This good for us."

"Yes it is, but what are we going to do about it?" I said.

"They use sword, then we use magic," Beeval said. "We kill."

For such a sweet demon, he had a seriously rock-hard side of him.

"What spells are you using?" I asked, kneeling down, keeping my eyes on the show outside.

"Killing spell. You have one?"

I sighed. "Yes."

"Then we use killing spell."

I didn't like to use them. Killing felt wrong. I'd had to do it a few times, and it never felt good. But in this case, perhaps I could get over myself, because Ashlar deserved it, if anyone did. That and I wanted to live.

"We are not here to discuss Desdemona—" Deirdre continued.

"You should be. It is because of the Desdemonas you will suffer. Had the elder of the line held to her end of the bargain, you would not be suffering." Ashlar smiled, and it was a terrible thing to see.

He really needed to brush his teeth. I could see that from here.

What did he eat, for goddess' sake?

"I don't know about that," Daniella said. "You didn't exactly honor the contract either."

Ashlar opened his mouth, and then closed it abruptly. "Are you questioning my word?"

"I am." Daniella nodded. "I have the contract here." She pulled the gross thing out of her waistband.

Eww. I hadn't even bothered to ask what had happened to the contract.

"In it, the agreement is to surrender the souls of Granny and Meema when they leave this Earth. Granny said you showed up on Meema's eighteenth birthday. That's not exactly when they leave this earth." She looked up from the contract.

"It is when I chose to have them leave the earth," Ashlar shot back.

"That wasn't in the contract."

Ashlar shrugged. "And?"

"So Granny didn't really break the contract. Because you broke it first."

Beeval hissed next to me. "Call the Big Boss."

"What?" I asked.

"The Big Boss. Handles disputes. Ashlar cheated. Big Boss decide."

"Holy shit," I breathed.

"Big Boss make Ashlar honor contract."

"What's Big Boss' name?" I asked.

Beeval's forehead wrinkled as he thought. "Sojin," he said finally. "His name Sojin. Call him now. We call him." Beeval grabbed my hands.

"I don't—Beeval—"

"*Thehruksh Sho'jin*!" Beeval yelled.

Oh sweet goddess. They were going to hear us. I chanted with Beeval as I snuck a look over the windowsill.

"I don't recognize this language," I whispered.

"Way we speak in Hell," Beeval said, and shouted out the chant again.

I couldn't believe I was hiding in the house while they were out there facing that greasy asshole.

"Beeval, let's go face him."

He stared up at me, his eyes wide with fear.

"I'll be with you," I said, standing and keeping hold of his hand.

He stopped speaking, then he nodded. "We call loud as we walk out. So he know. Once we call Big Boss, tell Ashlar we dispute, and want ruling."

"And he has to stop whatever he's doing?" I couldn't believe it was this easy.

Beeval nodded. "When a Big Boss has to settle, no one can do anything."

"Then let's go."

Hand in hand, we walked out onto the porch.

Deirdre whipped around, hearing us. "What are you two doing here? Get back in the house!" she hissed.

"Listen, and repeat," I said, trying to keep the explanations to a minimum. "Yell it for everyone in the back, Beeval."

He nodded, and raised his voice. "*Thehruksh Sho'jin*!" He repeated it, his voice loud.

I could see that Ashlar was stunned. He obviously hadn't expected this turn of events. And he was trying to see who was yelling for what was apparently his boss.

I joined in, nodding to my sisters, the Deanas, and Zane. Slowly, they began to repeat the unfamiliar-sounding words, and Beeval and I, still holding hands, stepped down off the porch to stand between Deirdre and Daniella.

"I have it ready," Deirdre said, touching the back of her neck.

I nodded, not stopping the chanting.

"What are you doing? There's no need for— who is that?" Ashlar took two steps toward our lawn, peering at Beeval. "Why do you have one of my demons?"

"He's not yours," I said, feeling the anger course through me. He probably didn't even know Beeval's name. "He is here of his own free will, at our invitation."

"You can't just steal away one of my demons!" Ashlar was outraged, which was kind of funny.

"I didn't. I invited him, and he came." I met his gaze.

"You will suffer for an age," Ashlar said to Beeval with no inflection at all.

The ground rumbled again. Beeval stopped chanting. "He is coming," he said, putting his hands on his hips and glaring at Ashlar. "You cheat, you answer to Sojin."

"I didn't cheat!" Now Ashlar looked not only pissed, but annoyed.

I hoped he was also feeling a little nervous. The prick.

"You better hope not," Daniella said. "There is honor even among demons. Your boss is going to be angry if you tried to cheat Granny and you're harassing us now."

"You do not know of what you speak," Ashlar said, crossing his arms. "We shall see."

"This is it?" DeAnna asked. "Why isn't he trying to kill us?"

"He can't. Apparently, when there's a contract dispute, all parties have to stop whatever bullshit they're trying." I glared at Ashlar.

"How did you come to leave my hospitality, Desdemona?" Ashlar asked conversationally. "Since I didn't plan to let you leave any time soon, I'm thinking my small demon there was a part of it?"

"I got myself out," I said, not willing to expose Beeval. "And I invited him."

"You are both going to suffer a great deal when this small hiccup is over," he said in the same conversational tone.

"So you say," Deana said. "I think you might have screwed up." She shook her head. "Sloppy."

"Maybe not poke the demon," Zane said. "Even if we have brief upper hand."

"Scared?" Daniella asked. "Poking is kind of our thing." She grinned.

"Yes," I said before Zane could answer. "I am. But Beeval said this is the way things are done, so I'm trusting him."

"Hope that doesn't go to shit," Dee said out of the side of her mouth.

The ground rumbled again. Out of the corner of my eye I saw Mrs. Kittrick, of all people. She was pruning her bushes, and the cats were twining around her feet. At the rumble, both Tinkie and Winkie stopped, and stared into our yard.

Mrs. Kittrick didn't even notice. The wards were holding, for the people at least.

I nodded to the cats. "Tinkie, Winkie! Get her inside!"

Both cats stared at me, and then casually strolled to the porch, meowing loudly. Mrs. Kittrick stood up, speaking to them. I couldn't hear what she said, but when both cats meowed and moved closer to the door, she put down her shears and followed them into the house.

A rolling black vapor, darker and more evil-smelling than the first plume came out of the crack and then a demon twice as tall as Ashlar and black as night appeared. He was gleaming, and his horns had to be six feet across. He was massive.

"Why have you called me?" He glanced around.

"Are you Sojin?" I asked politely. He seemed more annoyed than anything else, and I didn't want to piss him off.

"I am. Why do mortals wish for my presence? Why am I here, Ashlar?"

Ashlar bowed his head. "I believe the mortals wish to register a complaint."

"That is not unusual." Sojin looked over at the seven of us, apparently missing Beeval, his frown deepening. "Mortals often do. This is not for me to be concerned with." He turned from us, and moved a step back toward the crack in the road.

I wondered how in the hell—pardon the pun—we were going to cover the cracks up?

"Wait!" Deirdre called. "We called you because we do have a complaint. Ashlar was dishonest in his fulfillment of the agreement. He cheated the humans who bargained with him."

Sojin stopped. "Is this true, Ashlar? Do they believe you have not kept to your word?"

Ashlar shrugged. "Mortals always do. They whine about fairness when the contract between us was clear."

"No, it wasn't," I said, stepping forward. "It was very much unclear. And Ashlar wrote it that way, exercising his part in it in a manner that benefited only him. He was not honest with the human."

"Was it with one of you?" Sojin surveyed me, my sisters, the Deanas, and Zane. His eyes came to rest on Beeval. "You do not belong here, demon."

"I stay," Beeval said, his voice shaking a little. "Humans let me stay."

"Why?" Sojin asked.

"We have our reasons," I crossed my arms.

"The bargain was between me and their grandmother. The woman cheated me. I have come to extract payment." Ashlar brought things back on track.

"He cheated her, right from the beginning." Daniella interrupted.

Now Sojin just looked pissed. "Both sides are claiming the other cheated? Demons are free to do as they wish." He looked at all of us with more annoyance, and a helping of scorn.

"Really? Even break their word?" I asked. "Because you guys have enough problems anyway, with being evil. This joker hits all the stereotypes." I jerked my thumb at Ashlar. "I thought that a contract was binding once signed."

Sojin sighed loudly, and when he exhaled, the sour smell of brimstone filled my nose.

"God," Deana said. "They really do stink."

Dee covered her nose.

"Do you have the contract?" Sojin asked.

"We do," Deirdre said.

"Let me see it, mor—" He stopped, peering at us. "Not all of you are mortal. Ah. Witches." He glared at Ashlar. "You made a bargain with witches?" He shook his head. "Give me the contract, witch," Sojin finally finished his instruction to Deirdre, holding out a long arm that ended in massive hands and claws.

Deirdre walked forward, and handed him the contract. He read it silently. When he finished reading, he directed his words to Deirdre. "Where do you believe Ashlar has cheated?"

Ashlar made a noise of protest and Sojin held out a hand.

"He said that he would take their souls when they left this earth. That suggests when the body dies. The agreement was for immortality until the time my grandmother and mother chose to die. Ashlar showed up when my mother turned eighteen, and told my grandmother it was time to leave the earth. She said no, that's not what it said. He told her that leaving the earth could happen many ways, and that he'd decided it was time. That was not in the contract. He bent the rules."

"But your grandmother chose to die?"

"Not until some years later."

"The witch Desdemona didn't give me her and her daughter's souls! She gave me two other women instead!" Ashlar yelled. "She did not fulfill her end of the agreement."

"After you altered the terms of the agreement," Sojin said. "The claims of the witches have merit. Why have I been called in this matter?"

"He took me to Hell as payment for being cheated. He took our mother as well, and put her in the River of Souls. He told me that he would never stop being an asshole and bothering our family ever, not until we were all dead. So not only does he want payment, he's asking for interest, too! On a contract he screwed my grandmother over with!" I said loudly.

Ashlar's expression was murderous. I'm sure he wanted to kill us all, me in particular. He was like a powder keg ready to blow. But he'd been yelled at once by Sojin; he kept his mouth shut this time around.

"I believe I can solve this problem," another voice said.

We turned to see Granny's ghost drifting along the front porch.

CHAPTER TWENTY

"Desdemona!" Ashlar roared. "That is her! That is the cheat!" He took a few steps toward our lawn, and Sojin, who was reading over the contract once more, flicked a hand in his direction, which shoved Ashlar back.

"You are the Desdemona Nightingale who signed this?" he asked Granny.

She nodded. "I am."

"And were you expecting Ashlar to call on you when your daughter turned eighteen?"

"No." Granny shook her head. "I assumed we would choose when we'd die. When he showed up, I had no interest in dying."

"Who did you find to fulfill the bargain?"

"Two women who were dying. I agreed to help them in the manner they asked, and they agreed to go with Ashlar when he came."

"You didn't notice the difference between the witch and the mortals she supplied in her place?" Sojin cast a loaded glance at Ashlar, who paled under his boss' scrutiny.

"They all look alike, these mortals. Even witches," Ashlar said, but his defiance was not as prominent now.

"Sloppy," Sojin said. "Very sloppy. How did you get out of Hell?" he asked me.

"What? Oh, I was able to break free, and escape through a tunnel," I said.

"With no help?"

"I'm not stupid," I said, unwilling to sell out Beeval.

"No, apparently not," Sojin said, looking down at Beeval. He tapped his claws on the parchment. "What is your solution?" This was directed at Granny.

"My granddaughters have brought my spirit back. I will go with Ashlar now, on the condition that he leaves the rest of my descendants alone."

"You do not make terms!" Ashlar shouted.

"Be silent," Sojin snapped, and his eyes gleamed red. "I have been called here to settle a dispute. This means that I will decide what is to happen, and I will ask you for information as I need it." The raw power that rolled off his words made my heart speed up. The danger was palpable.

This greasy dumbass was going to get us all blown up.

Ashlar shut up.

The silence stretched out as Sojin read the contract a third time, and then stared off into the distance. His face was impassive, the red gleam gone from his eyes. Finally, he looked back at us, and then Ashlar.

"Here is my decision. While I cannot fault you for claiming your fee early, you did not state it in the agreed-upon bargain. That was your mistake. The woman was within her rights to attempt to subvert your interpretation of the contract since you wrote it poorly." He glared at Ashlar, who seemed to wilt down a foot.

"I do not like to give credit to the mortals, witches or no, but this one was smart and she provided you with two souls. The fact that they were not the specific souls you wanted—they were still two souls. And if you did not notice for many years, again, that is at your door. Now you have a third soul, part of the River, correct?"

Ashlar nodded. His fists were clenched by his sides, but he didn't speak.

"You have more than what you originally agreed upon. For your stupidity, you will not get the soul of the woman who signed." He nodded at Granny. "You have gotten more than you deserve, and this is your punishment for being stupid and allowing a human witch to outsmart you. You will no longer involve yourself with these humans. This bargain is fulfilled." He rolled up the parchment.

"Then the immortal life I gifted your descendants is no more!" Ashlar raised his hands.

"No!" Granny shrieked, her ghost moving in front of us to block whatever he was about to do. "No! They must be allowed to keep the immortal life! Take me! I'll go with him if he leaves things as they are!"

"No, witch! I shall suffer your cheating no longer!" Ashlar roared.

Deirdre, Daniella and I raised our hands. The magic swirled around us, and we were all ready to blast his greasy ass when Ashlar flew backwards, hitting a tree across the street from the house.

"I have made my decision," Sojin said. "You broke the bargain. Worse, you were foolish in how you managed things. You were defeated in your attempts to cheat by the human witch. Yet you still collected two souls, and now have a third. You will bother the humans no longer, and you will not alter anything that has already been given."

Holy shit.

"So now what?" DeAnna asked.

Sojin turned his gaze to her, and I could feel her fear rise off her. But she didn't move, or back away, and I was proud of her.

"We are done here. Ashlar, you will come with me. You will not return here. This matter is closed," Sojin said, moving to the crack in the road. He stopped. "Demon, if you choose to stay, you will not be able to return."

I didn't know what he was talking about until Beeval moved forward and bowed. "Master Big Boss, Beeval stay here. No go back."

"If that is your choice, then so be it." He turned his back to us, waving his hand to where Ashlar was sprawled against a tree. Ashlar floated past us, glaring with such hate that I wanted to shrink from it. But I forced myself to stay still, and with far less drama when they showed up, both of the demons disappeared into the crack.

The vapors followed, thank goddess, leaving only a lingering smell of brimstone.

"What in the hell just happened?" I turned to look at everyone else. "We didn't even need to use it!" I gestured at Deirdre.

"Into the house, girls," Granny said, her face worried. "I don't feel safe out here."

"We need to fix that crack first," Daniella said.

"Let's do it," I said, and the three of us, me, Daniella, and Deirdre, walked to the road. Together, we sent magic to the crack, sealing it from below. I didn't feel good with a crack to Hell right in front of the house, but there was nothing to do but close it up and hope for the best. Hope that it didn't become a tunnel or a shortcut out of Hell.

Once the road was sealed, we all went back into the house.

"We should probably call the city, and have them come and repair it. It looks like shit," Deirdre said.

"Put it on the to do list, tomorrow maybe?" Daniella laughed a little.

We joined her.

"I feel like more should have happened," Dee said. "That felt..."

"Anti-climatic?" Deana said.

"Yes!" I said. "It did. Like, I'm waiting for the other shoe to drop, or something, and Ashlar to show back up and say 'Nope, suckers!'"

"No," Beeval said, coming from the back of the house with Evil on his head. I hadn't even seen him come in and go searching for Evil, but there he was. "Once Big Boss decide, no one go against. Ashlar not strong enough. He gone."

"Really? You're sure?" Daniella asked. "He won't come back to bother us?"

"I don't think that Sojin really cared," Zane said. "I also don't think he liked Ashlar very much."

"You have to wonder if anyone likes that guy," Deana said, shaking her head. "Gross doesn't even begin to cover it." She faced me. "And you got away from him. Desdemona, that's amazing. I would have been scared into paralysis, or something."

"I was," I said. "He still scares me. He was going to hurt me badly, and he meant it." It would take a long time for me to stop seeing Ashlar's face looming over me, mocking and leering, smelling like a garbage dump.

"You're safe now," Daniella said, coming to hug me. Deirdre joined her. We stood together, holding on to one another. I felt the three of our nieces join us, and we all hugged. I knew what had happened, but it wasn't properly computing in my brain. I was shaking, still ready to attack, and I knew that I needed to get inside, and find a way to come down.

"We need to remove the wards," Deirdre said. "You up for it?" She looked at me.

"Yes," I said. I needed this.

Deirdre, Daniella and I stood shoulder to shoulder,

throwing up our hands to release the wards that surrounded not only our home but the town itself. Personally, I was all for leaving wards up at all times, but Meema had always said no, you didn't know what others were up to, and sometimes it wasn't as bad as we thought.

I was the most suspicious one of us. There was no denying that. Even more so after everything that had happened—oh, goddess. Just this week.

"I think I need to sleep for a month," I said.

"We need to talk to Granny," Deirdre said, glancing over to where Granny stood.

"Where's Doc?" I asked.

Granny turned, drifting a little. She didn't seem to have as much control over her ghost self as Doc did.

"He didn't want to watch this," she said, her expression sad. "He said that what he saw before when you and Desi disappeared was too difficult."

Deirdre opened her mouth but I laid a hand on her arm before she could speak. Doc seeing what had happened had changed over one hundred years of anger and resentment for him. It must have been really traumatic, and if he was going to be here, even if he was going to leave, I didn't want to fight with him. I wanted things right, no matter what happened.

"Fair enough," I said. "Let's get inside. The neighbors don't need to see you," I added. "They think we're weird enough as it is."

"Better than being husband stealers and homewreckers," Granny said, drifting into the house.

"Yeah, not so much on the husband stealing anymore," Daniella said. "Really, who wants anyone here?"

I glanced at Zane as she said that. He was also sneaking a side eye look at me, and we both looked away as fast as we could. I could feel my heart beat faster as heat flooded my cheeks.

Why did the only guy I'd found remotely attractive in decades have to be a necromancer? I was going through all the reasons in my head why this wasn't a good idea when Granny said, "Girls, there are things we need to speak of—"

"You think?" Deidre asked.

"I do," Granny said in the same tone Deirdre had used.

"I can't get over the ghosts being just like anyone else," DeAnna said from behind me.

"But I think that you—all of you—need sleep, and to rest before Doc and I speak with you."

"Are you getting married?" Deana asked, a laugh escaping from her.

"Bite your tongue, missy," Granny snapped. "This is far more important than romance," she added.

"Didn't you do a deal with a demon for romance? Or did I miss something?" Dee asked.

"You missed something," Granny said. "And I have been talking with Doc and he has persuaded me that there should be no more secrets. That I need to tell you all of my truth, all the things that have led us here."

"That would be a good thing, Granny. I have to ask, though—did Meema know?"

"No." Granny shook her head. "No one knew. Doc said you read my diaries?" Her face was hopeful, which was weird.

"Not all of them," Daniella said. "We were kind of in a time crunch."

Granny nodded. "Well, we'll need the diaries. But I am not kidding—you all need to go to sleep. You need to rest."

"So we don't slap the shit out of you when you tell us the real deal?" Deirdre asked.

"Hold your judgement," Granny said.

Doc appeared from the ceiling. "You all made it and are immediately venturing into the Nightingale family tradition of heated discussion?" He was smiling as he spoke.

"We're not at the heated part yet," I said. "But it's getting hot fast."

"I am pleased that you are all still here, and alive. I cannot express how relieved I am. But your grandmother is right. You do need rest."

"We're going to want to kill her, aren't we?" I asked Doc.

"I'm right here," Granny flared.

Doc sighed. "No, but you will not be happy. It's not a happy sort of tale. But you do need to hear it, and I think it will explain everything."

"How come the ghosts know everything?" Dee wondered.

"Because we can go anywhere— well, most of us can," Granny said, looking at Doc with a decidedly guilty expression. "We see a great deal."

"It's nice that you've decided to share. I'd like to hear it now," Deirdre said.

"So would I," I said in unison with Daniella, Dee, DeAnna, and Deana.

"You too?" Doc asked of Zane.

"I can't walk away from this now," Zane said.

Granny and Doc exchanged a glance, and then it was Granny's turn to sigh. "You girls sure you don't want to sleep?"

"No," all six of us—seven, if you counted Zane--said.

"Then sit down."

Everyone wandered into the kitchen, taking seats around the island, and bringing over chairs from the table. Dee moved to the fridge, and pulled out iced tea, and some cheese, and then some crackers and fruit. I was too tired, too worn, and too worried about what we were about to hear.

Deana and Dee poured glasses for everyone. It was funny that they were the ones doing this, in our house, but I liked it. They were family.

When everyone had a glass, Granny began. "When I moved here, I was infatuated with everything. Oh, you girls didn't know what it was like. It was a shadow of itself by the time you four were born. But Deadwood was alive, and for twenty-four hours a day, this town lived. It was intoxicating."

"Yeah, how did that happen?" Daniella asked. "How was it that Meema had four kids at the same time and lived?"

"Hold that question, Daniella. You'll understand in a moment."

Daniella nodded, crossing her arms. She was the most even-tempered of the three of us, but she was showing signs of anger, which was not good for the person on the receiving end. In this case, that would be Granny.

"I met Doc, and I was even more infatuated. We had so much fun! And then he told me that he was returning to Cheyenne. I loved him, at that time." She glanced at Doc, and he smiled.

It wasn't the smile of lovers; it was the smile of two people who had a history, and it was a long history that had found some peace. It was more friendly than anything else.

"My mother had taught me, before she died, some herbal lore, some ability to help using the plants she'd been taught by her grandmother. It wasn't much," Granny added. "I was only fourteen when she died. I turned fifteen right after her death. My father had died, or run off some years before, and my mother got cholera and died and left me an orphan. The church"—the corner of her mouth lifted in a small sneering twist—"that she'd attended took me in. The pastor was so nice, he and his wife were so pleased to be able to help me. I lived with them for a year. I'd just turned sixteen when the pastor attempted to visit me at night, after the household had gone to bed. It was my time to repay his kindness, he told me." She stopped, her eyes going faraway, and her eyes narrowed as the anger from all those years ago washed over her. "I told him that I was scared, and needed to think about it—and he told me to ready myself for him the next night. I snuck out of the house that night, taking all my clothing, and some of the good silver as well. What?" She looked at us. "As a woman with no money, I would have been nothing more than a camp girl somewhere. I knew that, even then. And I feel no shame from stealing from a would-be rapist." Granny sniffed.

"I can't believe you stole something," I said.

"Well, you get desperate. I'd already lived as a girl orphan for the past year. People's charity only goes so far, and they tend to feel you owe far more than you do. Like the pastor," Granny added.

"Well, I was able to hike through the woods, gathering herbs and staying off the roads. I needed to get far away before I tried to sell my silver. I had to get close to Kansas, because I couldn't sell it anywhere in the western part of Missouri." She looked down.

But she continued, "I sold it for a good price, and I was able to cobble together a ticket that got me to Rapid City. I wanted to go as far as I could from Missouri, and everyone was talking about Deadwood. This was before Custer," she added. "I got a stagecoach from Rapid City to Deadwood, and I was young, pert, and needed a job. I lied, and told the manager at the Bella Union that I was 18 and orphaned. That no one was trying to find me. He was fine with that, and I became a dancing girl. Some of the girls were more, of course, but I wasn't interested. Not until I met Doc." She smiled at Doc.

He returned the smile. "In my brief venture as a faro dealer, I made a realization despite the money to be made. It was far too cold for me to ever have been here for long, but once I met Desi, she helped me forget the cold for a spell."

I made a face. "That is definitely some history we do not need."

"Stop your filthy mind," Granny said. "We had fun, and he was the first person who wasn't trying to get something over on me. It was a nice change. He taught me cards when he realized I wasn't foolish, or a vapid woman. I am so grateful, because when Doc left, I was able to support myself. But before that, when Doc told me he was leaving." Granny pulled her story back on track. "I offered to help him. My mother had worked with people with consumption. I could have kept him living longer, although I couldn't have cured him."

"Which was news to me," Doc interjected. "I thought you had made the bargain when you made that offer."

Granny shook her head. "I did not. I wish I had, but that was not what drove me to make the bargain with Ashlar."

"What made you do that?" I asked. I forced myself to keep myself on track with her story. I had so many questions I wanted to ask, but I felt like there was something coming. Even though we'd just defeated Ashlar, and didn't have to use the angel sword, and now had that as an asset, although I wasn't sure what we'd use it for, I felt there was more. And that it was not going to be good news.

"Before I tell you, I have to tell you that I tried to tell you before. When I came back, I brought myself back. And I ran into Deana first, and blurted this all out. She left, after calling me awful names. Which I deserved. But I didn't want to have you three leave your mother. She was already so upset about Deana. It's all due to this." She pulled a ghost letter from inside her blouse. Granny looked so upset, and nervous, and like she was about to cry.

I wanted badly to know how it was possible for a ghost to be hanging onto a letter. See? I needed to focus.

Granny continued. "One more thing—" She held up a hand. "Wait. What is your full name?" she asked the Deanas.

"Why?" Dee asked.

"Humor me, please," Granny said.

"I am Deana," Dee said. "But I chose to go by Dee. My daughter is also Deana. I don't know why we insisted on naming ourselves after Gram, but we did."

"I'm DeAnna, but that's not my real name," DeAnna said.

"What is it?" Granny's face was frightened as she asked.

"Desdemona," DeAnna said. "Mom said she didn't know why she named me that—she loved you very much," she said to me, "but she wasn't sure what compelled her to do it. Afterwards, I asked her if I could change it up a little, because no one could ever spell my name." She rolled her eyes. "I legally changed it when I was eighteen."

"No, they never can," I said.

"Even after she knew," Granny said. "How could she? After she knew!"

"All right, stop with the damn drama," Daniella said. "Tell us what this is all about."

Granny sighed, and loOked at Doc. He nodded, giving her encouragement.

"I made the deal for immortality because right after your mother was born, I was informed I, and she, and anyone else of our name was cursed."

"Cursed how?"

"What are you talking about?"

"You don't think we needed to know this before now?"

"Are we cursed even if we didn't grow up here?"

We all had questions that flew at her, and Granny held up her hands in a 'Stop' motion. "One question at a time. I cannot answer all at once. To begin with, I went into the bargain hoping to break the curse on your mother and me. When I began to worry the curse would affect you girls, I came back to see your mother. That's when I saw Deana." Granny stopped.

Even as a ghost, she was overcome by emotion.

"What was the curse?" Zane asked.

She waved the letter a little. "That all the Desdemonas have to die."

EPILOGUE

Ashlar paced his quarters, his hooves clacking on the stone floor. Shadows flickered from torches on the wall. He couldn't sit still; couldn't contain himself. He'd been humiliated.

Bad enough that it was at the hand of humans. Worse that the humans used Sojin to deliver the shame.

Word of his disgrace had traveled far and wide throughout the realms of Hell. He was all but ruined. No one would work with him. His power, his word, his reputation—it was near to gone. The demons who worked for him were restless, teetering on mutiny. This situation could not go on.

He would need to do something. He had to gain his position back, or he would be no better than the little rat that had run to the humans. He might as well run to the humans himself and beg for mercy and shelter.

That would never happen. He would not falter. This merely required a new plan, one that would show even when he was driven down, he did not fall.

"Get in here!" he bellowed.

A small demon scuttled in, head down. "Master?"

"Find me Madigan," Ashlar said.

The demon hesitated. "Madigan, master?"

"Yes. Hurry," he added with a snarl. What was next? The minion demons refusing to do as they were told?

That would not happen.

Madigan, for all his faults and mistakes would be perfect for what he had in mind.

In a longer amount of time than was acceptable, Madigan strolled in. Madigan was a half-human, half-demon breed, and as such, he could shift from his demon form to human form. He was seen as lesser due to his half-human lineage, but for this, he would be perfect.

"How are ya, Ashlar? Little lonely?"

"Your attitude does not help you," Ashlar said.

"Look, I'm no saint." Madigan grinned at the joke. "But my boss didn't haul my ashes in front of humans."

Ashlar waited, and then said, "Are you finished?"

Madigan tapped his chin. "Yeah, I think I am."

"Good. I have an assignment for you."

"What do I get?" Madigan asked. "You're not exactly good currency right now. You could bail on me, leave me high and dry."

"Are you questioning me?" Ashlar asked, even though he knew why Madigan asked. Madigan wasn't the sort you called in for an above-board job. He was a behind the scenes, keeping things quiet kind of demon.

"Yeah, I am. It's a fair question. You know it, I know it, all of Hell knows it."

Ashlar reined in his temper. He didn't tolerate disrespect, but there was something to be said for Madigan's straightforward questions. It was one of the reasons he'd kept the half-demon around all these years.

"You will not be left high and dry,"

"But?" Madigan asked with one raised brow.

"This must be kept quiet."

"I figured. You're going after them, aren't you?"

"Why should I not?"

"Oh, I don't know." Madigan tapped his chin, looking up at the ceiling. "Because your boss told you to step off and sit down? I don't like rules, but Sojin is nothing to mess with."

"I am breaking no rules. I want you to look in on the youngest human that was there. A woman named Deana Holliday."

"Isn't she one of the family you were told to leave alone?"

"I am doing nothing. You are doing nothing. I want you to watch her, see what she is doing. She is several generations removed from the original Desdemona, but she has the spark of the other witches in the family."

Madigan sighed. "You know, boss, you might want to let this one go."

No one else could speak to him that way. Ashlar knew that Madigan was being honest, with no agenda at hand. That was rare, in Hell. "I can no longer seek retribution from the Desdemonas. Deana Holliday is not a Desdemona."

Madigan said, "Boss—"

"Enough. I have heard your concerns. But I am offering you an assignment. Will you take it or no?"

Madigan put his hands in his pockets and looked up, thinking. "Yeah. I'll do it. You leave me solo, and I'll move around and talk more than I usually do."

"Understood."

"And it will cost you."

"Very well."

"Give me the details," Madigan said.

Ashlar walked to the other side of the room, willing the memories that he had stored to come forth.

No human had ever bested him, and he would not allow that to change. Not now. Not ever.

He shared the thoughts with Madigan. The other demon considered them quietly.

"Well?" Ashlar struggled to contain his impatience.

"I'll do it," Madigan said. "But if I'm found out, it's on you."

"Understood. We are agreed?"

Madigan nodded.

Ashlar held out his hand, gesturing for Magidan to do the same. The dark-haired man gave his hand over, almost reluctantly, and then winced as Ashlar pressed their palms together.

As he watched, the sigil flared on Madigan's palm. Brighter and brighter it burned, and it pleased Ashlar to see that Madigan was gritting his teeth. That's what he got for showing up here in human form.

Abruptly, the sigil went dark. It was no longer visible, but it was there, ready to be called forth when the bargain was complete.

"Go," he said to Madigan.

Rubbing his palm, Madigan left without a word.

Ashlar turned away, considering all the ways he could achieve his goals. Then he laughed.

In the tunnel, Madigan winced as the harsh sound echoed off the walls of Hell.

TRANSLATIONS

Latin Phrases:

Peregrinatione ad angustos - Keep within this block/ward
Daemon ignis – Demon fire
Praefundo – Wet before the fire
Victa - Conquered
Praesidio - Protection
Supra et infra spiritibus
nostrae vocationis audiat
Ad eos qui nos ad pallii
Salvos nos fac Domime O spirituum,
Nos atque piae.
Deferrent nostrae
Sine ulla peccatum.
Spirits above and below
Hear our call
Bring to us those who
Have moved to the pall.
Keep us safe, oh spirits,
Us and our kin.

Bring them to our light
Without any sin.

Quadrato autem dicamus, Ashlar.
Precipimus tibi quod ostendam tibi, et stare ante nos -
Ashlar, we call you. We command you to come before us.

Demon Phrases:

Kaabe't'aek shu'eshak - Souls come to me
Thehruksh Sho'jin - Come forth Lord Sojin

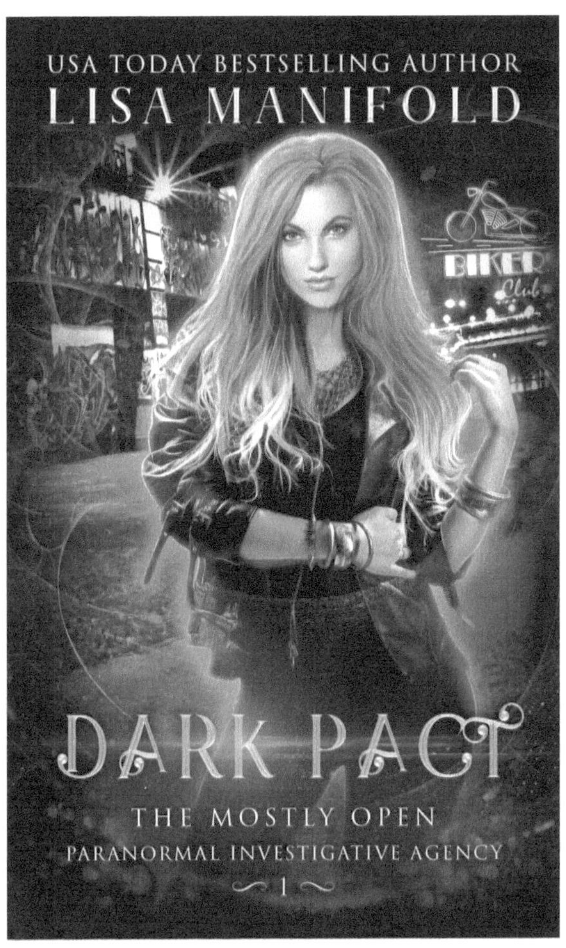

In Hellborn, you met the Deanas, the descendants of Deana, one of the Deadwood Sisters. The youngest, Deana Holliday (not to be confused with DeAnna, her Gran, or Dee, her mom), has lived in Venice, California all her life in an old house on one of the canals. She returns from Deadwood ready to start her life in a new direction, which means leaving all she's ever known. Things don't always go the way she plans.You can find the first book, Dark Pact,

by clicking HERE or on Amazon.

ACKNOWLEDGMENTS

I don't always do these. The people close to me know who they are, and what they mean to me.

But it's a little different with this book.

First, my thank you to the voluminous work by dedicated authors and historians out there on John Henry "Doc" Holliday. While the Doc in my book is based on history's records of him, I've taken liberties with the man I chose to create. I first found him when my husband and I went to Tombstone, and I read everything I could get my hands on after that visit. The allure of that time in our history has never waned for me.

Along with that, I wanted to share that there really is a house on Pearl Street. It really started out life on Main Street, and was moved in the last twenty years. I've seen the pictures, and it's a gorgeous place. I wanted my Deadwood sisters to have a house like them—one with history, longevity, and the ability to grow, move and change (but only within the city limits of Deadwood!). It's all they've ever known, which means "home" can be both a blessing and a curse.

Second, thank you to Kim Cunningham from Atlantis Book Design. Her covers are always a temptation, and when I saw this one, I knew this was Desdemona. She's gifted, and you'll see her art in the rest of the series.

Third, thank you to my writing partner, Corinne O'Flynn. I'm a better writer because I'm fortunate enough to have her as a colleague.

Fourth, to my crew of fellow inkslingers: Lori, Alex, Nathan, Stephanie, Andre, Bernadette. When you find your tribe of people, you know it.

Fifth, to my amazing husband and even more amazing children. You all are my rock, and I love you beyond belief.

A special nod to my son, Cooper. He wrote the demon language for me, and made sure that my Latin was what he calls 'vulgar'. I didn't want it to be formal, and he said I did a good job managing that. (Yay, me!) In addition to the demon language, which is far more intricate than the small phrases seen in this work, he created Ashlar's sigil, and I LOVE it.

Seventh, to my amazing editor, Zoe at Peppermint Editing. She asks the right questions, and points out the things that need to be addressed. She makes my words better. Of course, I'm the last person who puts their mitts on said words, so any mistakes still there are mine.

Finally, to my readers. You all have been with me since the beginning, since Thea and Casimir. Or Iris and Brennan. Or Tibby. Or Eamonn and Marigold. And I am so, so thankful! With Desdemona, and my Deadwood Sisters, I'm finding the joy of a new series and a new book family that writing has always given me. I'm so excited to share this world with you!

Lisa Manifold

April, 2019

ABOUT THE AUTHOR

Lisa Manifold is a *USA Today* Bestselling Author of fantasy, paranormal, and romance stories. She moved to Colorado as an adult and has no plans of living anywhere else. She is a consummate reader, often running late because "Just one more page!" She is a fan of all things Con, and has an entire room devoted to the costumes created for Cons.

Lisa is the author of many flavors of paranormal series, including The Realm, Djinn Everlasting, Dragon Thief, The Aumahnee Prophecy, Tales from the Veil, Sisters of the Curse, the books written with The Midnight Coven collective, the Deadwood Sisters and The Mostly Open Paranormal Investigative Agency.

She lives as close to the mountains as possible with her husband, children, and four red rescue dogs.

Stay in touch:
Sign up for Lisa's Newsletter and never miss a thing!
Website: www.lisamanifold.com
Or one of the links below.

ALSO BY LISA MANIFOLD

Vampire Mates

(with The Midnight Coven)

Immortal Darkness (Aug 2019)

The Mostly Open Paranormal Investigative Agency

Dark Pact

Dark Night (Oct 2019)

Vampire Brides

(with The Midnight Coven)

Forever Blood

Deadwood Sisters

Hellborn: The Unlucky Book 1

Hellfire: The Unlucky Book 2 (Sept 2019)

Dragon Thief

Dragon Lost

Dragon Found

The Realm Series

Heart of the Goblin King

To Wed the Goblin King

Realms of the Goblin King

Rise of the Dragon King

The Companion Tales, Volume I

The Companion Tales, Volume II

The Aumahnee Prophecy

with Corinne O'Flynn

Eamonn's Tale

Marigold's Tale

Watchers of the Veil

Defenders of the Realm

Tales From The Veil

with Corinne O'Flynn

The Portal Keepers

The Gimcrackers

Djinn Everlasting

Three Wishes

Forgotten Wishes

Hidden Wishes

Sisters of the Curse

Thea's Tale

One Night at the Ball

Casimir's Journey

Do you like being in the loop? Sign up for Lisa's newsletter! Shenanigans, book recs, and the latest news abound!

www.ingramcontent.com/pod-product-compliance
Lightning Source LLC
Chambersburg PA
CBHW022146240626
47153CB00007B/2538

* 9 7 8 1 9 4 5 8 7 8 1 5 2 *